# DYING TO KNOW YOU

ALSO BY AIDAN CHAMBERS

The Dance Sequence
*Breaktime*
*Dance on my Grave*
*Now I Know*
*The Toll Bridge*
*Postcards from No Man's Land*
*This is All: The Pillow Book of Cordelia Kenn*

*The Present Takers: a children's novel*
*The Kissing Game: a collection of short stories*

AIDAN CHAMBERS

# DYING TO KNOW YOU

THE BODLEY HEAD

DYING TO KNOW YOU
A BODLEY HEAD BOOK 978 0 370 33236 9

Published in Great Britain by The Bodley Head,
an imprint of Random House Children's Books
A Random House Group Company

This edition published 2012

1 3 5 7 9 10 8 6 4 2

The Random House Group Limited supports the Forest Stewardship Council (FSC®),
the leading international forest certification organization. Our books carrying the FSC
label are printed on FSC®-certified paper. FSC is the only forest certification scheme
endorsed by the leading environmental organizations, including Greenpeace. Our paper
procurement policy can be found at www.randomhouse.co.uk/environment.

RANDOM HOUSE CHILDREN'S BOOKS
61–63 Uxbridge Road, London W5 5SA

www.kidsatrandomhouse.co.uk
www.totallyrandombooks.co.uk
www.randomhouse.co.uk

Addresses for companies within The Random House Group Limited
can be found at: www.randomhouse.co.uk/offices.htm

THE RANDOM HOUSE GROUP Limited Reg. No. 954009

A CIP catalogue record for this book is available from the British Library.

Printed and bound in Great Britain by CPI Group (UK), Croydon, CR0 4YY

TO SUSAN VAN METRE

DYING TO KNOW YOU

# one
- - - - - -

"COULD I TALK TO YOU?"

"Why?"

"You're a writer?"

"And?"

"I need your help."

"You see the sign on the door?"

"Yes."

"What does it say?"

"No visitors without appointment."

"Have you an appointment?"

"No."

"Then I suggest you make one."

"Could I make an appointment?"

"When for?"

"Now."

I couldn't help laughing. Anyway, there was something about him, an indefinable quality that instantly appealed.

"What sort of help do you want?"

"With my girlfriend."

"I don't know anything about you, never mind your girlfriend."

"I can explain."

"Young man. I'm seventy-five. Happily married for over forty years. What would I know about girls these days?"

"You write about them."

"You've read my books?"

"No."

"So how do you know?"

"My girlfriend told me. She's a fan. And I looked you up on the internet."

"Really? Well, at least you're honest. But in any case, the girls in my books are fictions. I made them up. They don't have minds of their own. Real girls do."

"The help is just for me, really. Not my girlfriend."

"Look, if we're going to continue this conversation, which it seems we are, you'd better come inside."

Rooms are a fixed size, which can't be altered without pulling down walls and building new ones. They should be unchanging in shape and proportions. But sometimes they do change depending on who's in them.

I led him into the sitting room. He was tall, well built

but not bulky, not overbearing. I was surprised, because the room didn't shrink as it usually did when visitors came in. It got larger.

When we'd sat down, he on the edge of the sofa, leaning forward, elbows on knees, eyes looking at his hands clasped as if in prayer, me in the armchair facing him, I asked again how he thought I could help.

"My girlfriend wants me to write about myself," he said.

"And?"

"About myself. Inside."

"What? You mean your feelings?"

"My inner secrets, she said."

"Why?"

"She quoted something at me."

"Can you remember it?"

"'How can you call them friends when they do not know their mutual feelings.'"

"That's good. Did she say who said it?"

"Aristotle."

"Aristotle? She's read Aristotle?"

"No idea."

"Maybe she picked it up from the internet."

"She does read a lot. She'd like it here," he added, looking at the shelves of books.

"How old?"

"Seventeen."

"She's some girl, if she's read Aristotle."

"Well, yes, she is."

3

"Or maybe she's just good at finding quotes." I let that sink in before I said, "So what do you want me to do?"

"Help me write the stuff she wants."

"Why can't you write it yourself?"

"Hate writing."

"Then don't."

"She says she'll only go on with me if I do. She's made a list of questions she wants me to answer. And I have to do it in what she calls full-dress English."

"'Full-dress'?"

"Yes. Proper punctuation, spelling and stuff. And printed out. I hate doing that. It's torture."

"Not that bad, surely?"

"Yes, it is. And, anyway, I don't know what to write."

"What do you want me to do, then? Make it up?"

"No! . . . But that wouldn't be such a bad idea, come to think of it."

He looked at me and smiled for the first time and said, "Only joking. But still . . ."

"Still what?"

"Dunno . . . Well, I do, to be honest. There's a problem."

"Which is?"

He examined his hands again, fiddled with his fingers, took in a breath, and gave me a defiant look.

"I'm dyslexic."

"Ah!" I said. "I see."

Defiance turned to apology. "I have trouble writing. Not reading so much. But writing. Things get jumbled.

Not just letters and words. The sentences and the thoughts as well. Something happens between what's in my head and what comes out when I try to write it down. It's torture."

"Your parents know about this, and your teachers, of course?"

"My parents, and the teachers did when I was at school."

"You're not at school?"

"No."

"How old are you?"

"Eighteen."

I'd have said sixteen.

"What do you do for a living?"

"I'm training to be a plumber."

"I see. What's your name, by the way?"

"Karl. Karl Williamson."

"Haven't I seen you around?"

"We did some work in a house up the road not long ago. I used to go past your house. You were in the garden a couple of times."

"I thought I'd seen you. And your girlfriend, what's her name?"

"Fiorella. Fiorella Seabourne."

"Fiorella. Unusual name."

"Italian. Her mother's Italian."

"And she understands? About your dyslexia."

"She doesn't know."

"You haven't told her?"

"No."

"Then tell her."

"Not yet."

"Why not?"

"Don't want to."

"That's not good enough. If I'm going to help, you have to level with me."

He sat back, deciding, I think, whether he wanted to go on with this, after all. Then:

"Like I said, she's a big reader. And a big writer as well. Always at it. She wrote to you once. An email."

"Really? Did I answer?"

"Yes."

"You've read it?"

"No. Fiorella told me about it. She said she asked about being a writer and you told her that real writers read a lot of the best stuff ever written and write something every day, it doesn't matter what. You said writing a book was the most difficult thing you had ever tried to do and told her to do something else unless she was passionate about it."

"Did I? I can only say, if I did, I am in complete agreement with myself."

He laughed.

Karl was no glamour boy. But even during this first meeting I discovered he had something better. The kind of intelligence that's more attractive than physical beauty.

"Let me guess," I said. "You're afraid Fiorella will give up on you if she finds out you're dyslexic, because she'll think you're stupid."

"Something like that."

"In which case, why bother? She's not worthy of you."

He ignored the criticism and the compliment. I'm always interested in what people ignore in a conversation, especially when talking about their problems. The question is: Did they take in what was being said? Or didn't they want to hear it? This time, Karl's eyes shifted from mine, and looked down at his hands, now clenched between his knees.

"So why don't you tell Fiorella about it?"

"I don't want to tell her till she knows me better."

"How long have you been seeing each other?"

"Three months."

"Not long."

"Long enough."

"Long enough for what?"

"For me to know I want to hang on to her."

I let that pass. I knew exactly what he meant.

"She'll be bound to find out sometime. What then?"

"Dunno. I'll deal with it when it happens."

Not wise. But I needed time to think it over.

"What do you do in your spare time?" I asked.

"Fish. Play rugby. Play chess. Cook."

"So," I said, "you like facts and doing practical things, but aren't too keen on talking about your feelings."

"Something like that."

"OK. Let me sum up and you can tell me if I've got it right. You've met a girl you admire and would like to

7

keep her as your girlfriend. She fancies you and she wants to know about your private life, your intimate self, because she believes that real friends—let's say, lovers— tell each other about their secret selves. And she insists on you writing this. But you don't even like talking about yourself, and writing would be torture because of your dyslexia. So you've come to me, who you know nothing about except that I write books Fiorella likes. And you want me to help you by writing for you what she wants you to write for her in proper English. Is that it?"

"That's about it, yes."

"Good. Which leaves us with a couple of questions. One: Why should I help you? And two: If I help you, what is it you want me to write, exactly?"

"I don't know."

"You don't know what?"

"The answer to both questions."

I laughed.

"You must be desperate."

Karl laughed too. "I am!"

There was one of those pauses when neither can think what to say next. In the silence, an intuitive shift, felt rather than thought, occurs in knowledge of the other.

Karl looked awkward. In the silence, this moment of sudden awkwardness was like a door opening just enough to allow a glimpse into a room meant to be kept secret. I

8

saw that what it kept hidden was shyness and that Karl's brusqueness was a front, a carapace against discovery.

I knew this was true because it was like looking at myself.

And this, combined with the attraction of his intelligence, gave me the answer to one of the two questions that Karl couldn't answer. Why should I help him?

Because helping him was like helping myself when I was his age and helping myself with my own difficulties now.

I wondered what Karl was thinking of me.

"How about a coffee?" I said, to break the impasse. "Or something else?"

"If you like," he said, torn, I guessed, between the impulse to cut and run and his overriding need to obtain what he'd come for.

I led him to the kitchen.

Rooms change their shape according to who is in them, and there are rooms in which you feel more comfortable than in others.

For me, there are two. My workroom, the only place where, when I am alone, I am entirely myself, and because of this is a sacred room where I take very few people. And the kitchen—another workroom, now that I think of it—where I can be at ease when talking to visitors.

Karl sat at the table while I made coffee, asking him no more than the ritual how strong, with milk or without, sugar or not, and would he like a biscuit? I was pleased to see that he visibly relaxed. Another kitchen man, perhaps?

"You say you cook?" I asked as I gave him a mug of coffee and a chocolate ginger biscuit.

"Yes," he said. "You?"

"It relaxes me after a day's work. People think writing is what my father used to call head work. And it is, partly. But it's gut work as well. You live in your guts everything that happens in the story. Or at least I do. After a day of it my guts are tied in knots. Cooking helps to undo them. Who taught you?"

"School. Took it as an option."

"Lucky you. Boys weren't given the option in my day. What do you like most about it?"

"You don't have to write anything."

We laughed.

"And," he went on, "it's useful. You're making something people need and they like. Or they do if you get it right and do it well."

"You like getting things right and doing them well?"

He gave me a shy glance.

"Don't you?"

"Yes. And you know what I like about cooking? The tools. You don't use many tools as a writer. Pencils, pens, paper. A computer, of course, though I never think of it as a tool, only as a machine. My father was a joiner. Very skilled woodworker. He had lots of tools. I loved to watch him use them. All sorts of hammers, chisels, saws, awls, screwdrivers. He had some special knives. He had drills and clamps and punches and files. All of them with their own places to be, hanging on the wall in front of his bench or in his toolboxes. Planes, for instance, rasps, pliers, spanners, a set square, rulers. Lovely. All of them a bit worn and shiny from use. I thought they were beautiful. Still do. Not to mention the wonderful smell of wood. Well, cooking is a bit like that. Plenty of attractive tools to play with, and, as you say, something useful to make with them."

He nodded.

"Sorry," I said. "Carried away by nostalgia."

"Copper pans," he said with a grin. "I have a thing about copper pans."

"I can see why."

"I've a couple of saucepans, an omelette pan, and a copper bowl. I'd quite like some gratin dishes. Did you know that copper was the first metal used for making tools? That's because you can find it naturally, in the ground. It doesn't have to be made like iron or steel. It's the only metal that's like that."

"Really? I didn't know."

"And it's good for cooking because copper heats up quicker than any other metal used for cooking, and it heats up evenly all over the surface. The best pots are thick and heavy. Which is nice as well."

"They look lovely too, don't they? A beautiful colour, and shiny."

"But you have to polish them to keep them shiny. We use a lot of copper pipe in plumbing. I like bending it and soldering the joins."

He became aware of himself and shrugged.

We smiled at each other and were silent.

Another shift had happened.

I was beginning to see what Fiorella might see in him.

"Getting back to Fiorella," I said after a while.

He frowned.

"Have you written anything to her? You said she gave you some questions. Have you answered any of them?"

"Yes. But I tore it up. It was crap."

"Pity. Look, if I'm going to help you, I have to have something to go on. I can't make it up, now can I, seriously?"

"No. I know."

"The best I could do is turn what you've written into proper English—punctuation, grammar, spelling, that sort of thing—and maybe help you with the expression. But if I do more than that, well, we'd both be perpetrating a deception, wouldn't we? A lie."

He nodded.

I could see Fiorella's problem. Getting anything out of him was like squeezing juice from a stone.

I tried another tack.

"How often do you see each other?"

"Once a week mostly. She's studying for exams, and I do quite a lot of overtime. In my job you have to go to people's

12

houses in the evening when they're at home from work. So it's hard for us to meet except at weekends."

"Doesn't live near you?"

"No."

"You have transport?"

"Only a bike. Don't have a license. Keep failing the theory."

"Why? It's not that difficult, is it?"

A blank stare.

"Ah yes. Of course. Sorry!"

I cleared the mugs away, and leaned against the kitchen bench while I thought what to say next. I'd had enough for today.

"I'll tell you what. Why don't you bring Fiorella's questions to me tomorrow? I'll look through them and we'll talk some more. Maybe I can work out what to do when I see what she is asking. How does that sound?"

He took a moment before saying, "OK. What time? I'll be at work till sixish."

"Would eight suit you?"

"OK."

"Eight tomorrow, then, with Fiorella's questions."

He followed me to the front door.

"Thanks," he said, as he went past me. But stopped on the doorstep, and said, "Could I ask you something?"

"Sure."

"Why are you helping me?"

I gave him a wry look.

"Because you asked."

"That's all?"

"Perhaps one good turn deserves another?"

"Tit for tat."

"Quid pro quo."

"You scratch my back and I'll scratch yours."

"Not exactly what I had in mind."

"Don't see how I can help *you*."

"Time will tell."

I waved a salute and closed the door before he could say anything else.

# TWO

-------

I SEARCHED THROUGH MY FOLDER OF READERS' EMAILS AND FOUND Fiorella's. Sent the year before, when she said she was sixteen. The passage that caught my eye was this:

> I'm not much of a talker, though I often wish I were. So writing is very important to me. It's like a sleepover, when you feel you can say all kinds of things, because the darkness hides your blushes.
>
> I think there is no better way to get to know someone than reading what they write. Even if I lived with someone I loved, I'd still want to write to him all the time, and him to me.
>
> I don't have a boyfriend at the moment. I have only had a few. Three, to be exact. They were all pretty useless. None of them was any good at writing. I live in hope!

In one of your stories, a girl wrote that she lives to read and writes to live the life she cannot live otherwise. Is that true for you as well? I hadn't thought of it before, but I think it is true for me too.

Some of my friends say I'm a bit weird for reading and writing so much and taking it so seriously. In my opinion, they are the ones who are weird for not taking it seriously. Do you agree?

And do you have any tips that will help me to become a professional writer, because there is nothing else I want to be.

I tried to put myself in Karl's shoes by remembering myself at eighteen, when I was as shy and unrevealing as him, and drafted a letter he might send to Fiorella to keep her happy while he and I worked out what to do about the questions she'd set him.

Dear Fiorella [or Hi, Fiorella, or any salutation you prefer],

I've read your questions.

Do you really want to torture me?

If so, you're going the right way about it.

Like I told you, writing isn't my favourite thing.

But you've given me this ultimatum.

I think you're testing me, to see how much I want you.

Answer: Very much.

So I'll do it. Or I'll try.

But don't expect me to be quick. Answering all your questions could take a book. I have to think what I want to say and I am a slow writer.

I will send you a few answers, maybe just one at a time so you don't have to wait and get tired of waiting and ditch me anyway.

Is that OK?

Love [or whatever valediction you prefer],

Karl

# THREE

- - - - - - -

|

Karl arrived on the dot of eight.

"You're prompt."

"Don't like to be late."

"And don't like to be kept waiting."

"No."

"Nor me. A man of the clock."

We smiled agreement.

He was washed and brushed up. Long-sleeved black crewneck sweatshirt, well-fitting jeans, Merrell Urbino shoes, short, jet-black hair gelled into spikes a hedgehog would have been proud of.

He asked for a beer. I didn't have any, as I hate the stuff. So he settled for a glass of red wine. We sat as before in the kitchen. I was glad to see he relaxed at once.

He read my draft letter while I looked through Fiorella's questions, a list of more than fifty on two pages. And a set of six index cards on which Karl had organised the questions into topics, one topic to a card: Likes and Dislikes, Beliefs, Aims and Plans, Fiorella and Me, Love and Sex, Interests and Activities.

I asked him what he thought of the letter.

He gave me an assessing look.

"I'm a writer," I said. "I'm used to people telling me they don't like what I've written. Speak your mind."

He shrugged. "It's all right as a letter."

"But?"

"It's not. Not *me*, if you know what I mean."

"Not the way you'd have expressed it."

He nodded.

"OK. Let's have a go at it later. What about these questions? The answers would fill a book."

"That's what I said."

"And she said?"

"Write a chapter at a time."

"She has high expectations."

"About everything."

"And you like this about her?"

"Yes."

"Like her. Or love her?"

He blushed and frowned at his hands bunched round the glass on the table.

Too soon for such a question.

"Look," I said quickly. "Why don't you tell me how you met?"

He sat back, heaved a sigh like a boy being made to do his homework but knowing there was no way out of it, and pushed himself to begin.

"I was on a job with my boss. Putting a new bathroom in a granny flat at Fiorella's house. We were finishing the second fit. Most times we'd been there the granny was around. Both Fiorella's parents have full-time jobs so they're out all day, and Fiorella was at school. But it was her half-term holiday. The granny wanted to go out. Fiorella was told to see we were OK. She wasn't that bothered and kept out of the way."

"But you'd seen her before and liked what you'd seen?"

"Didn't take much notice. She was just a schoolgirl. And she hadn't taken any notice of me. I thought she was a bit stuck-up."

"And this was what? Three months ago?"

"Three months and a week today."

"So what happened next?"

"My boss got an emergency call from one of our regulars. An old lady who lives on her own. He rushed off to deal with her and left me to get on. Which only meant clearing up because we'd nearly finished. He told me to wait till he came back to check everything was OK."

"Let me guess. You cleared up, called for Fiorella to tell her you were finished and Eros struck."

I was glad he felt confident enough to laugh.

"Except it was chess."

"*Chess?*"

"Chess."

"How does chess come into it?"

"She said would I like to wait in the kitchen and have a cup of coffee. I felt a bit embarrassed. I'd seen a chess set when she took me through the living room to the kitchen. I play chess. So for something to say I asked her if she played. She said she did and would I like a game? Do you play?"

"Sorry, no."

"You should. It's a good game."

"I'm not a games player. To my mind, there are enough chances to fail in life without inventing more. But I've always liked the look of the pieces."

"Me too. That's what attracted me at first."

"When was that?"

"My . . . At school, when I was eleven. And another reason I like it"—a wide smile—"you don't have to write anything. And you don't talk while you're playing because you have to concentrate, which was useful that first time with Fiorella."

"Who won?"

"We hadn't finished when my boss came back. It was pretty even between us."

"And you agreed to meet again to finish?"

"Yes."

"Who suggested that?"

"Fiorella."

"So she made the first move."

He smiled. "White always makes the first move."

"She's blonde?"

"Sort of. Strawberry blonde."

"You met again. Where?"

"Her house."

"When?"

"Next day."

"Who won?"

"She did."

"You were nervous?"

"Well, she *is* good."

"What else?"

"What else did we do? Nothing. Talked chess. Played through a famous game just for fun. She has quite a lot of books on chess. Then she suggested some matches, three games a match starting at the weekend."

"So it was chess brought you together and kept you together. What's the score now?"

"Three to two in her favour. And two draws."

"But you must have done other things as well?"

"She watched me play rugby a couple of times. Last two games of the season."

"Who do you play for?"

"Nothing special. Highwood."

"But they're pretty good, aren't they? Always on the local news."

"Not too bad. You follow the game?"

"Sorry! I'm no more a rugby man than a chess man."

"Fiorella's not interested, either. But she likes tennis, so we've started playing that."

"Doing any better than at chess?"

"Two to one in my favour."

"I see one of her questions is why you like rugby so much."

"Tried to explain, but she can't understand it."

"Maybe that's a question we could start with? You know what you want to say. It shouldn't be too difficult."

"If you like."

"OK, let's do it. I'll take some notes while we talk. Then I'll write what you tell me. You can comment and we'll revise to suit you. And when you're happy with it, I'll print it out and you can give it to Fiorella. How about that?"

||

My summary of Karl's answers to my questions about why he likes rugby so much:

I like rugby because it's physical. So are football and hockey. But they aren't physical the same way as rugby. Rugby is a contact sport. I like that. Boxing is as well. But the aim is to hurt your opponent. Rugby can be pretty tough, you might say it's violent at times, but you aren't trying to hurt anybody.

It's skilled. You have to use all your skills of the body and the mind. Like chess, you have to think ahead three or four moves. It's a game of strategy and tactics. It's violence used with moral intelligence, if that makes any sense.

It's also fast. It exhausts you. Rugby releases the tensions and pent-up energy that have built up during the week at work. I like leaving a match feeling I've got rid of all the energy that has been locked up inside me. I have to be careful at work, because if I make a mistake it can be a disaster. But in rugby I can let myself go, drive hard, really go for it, and it doesn't matter if I get it wrong, it's only a game. Not that I like getting it wrong. That's not what I'm saying. I'm only saying that I can let myself go while I'm playing.

You can only win at rugby if everyone plays their part and works with the others. People who are only out for themselves, trying to score on their own and be the star, are looked down on. It's a terrific feeling when a move goes totally right, like a combination of passes, or a tackle, or a kick that are spot on. It's as if I'm part of a perfectly functioning machine. It's like music in motion. Almost like dancing. Not that I can dance!

Rugby is a dirty game. I like getting covered in mud and then cleaning it off afterwards. There's something very primitive about it. In fact, now

I come to think of it, there's something very primitive about rugby as a game.

It's so obvious that I won't bother to mention that rugby is good exercise. And it helps to keep me fit.

III

"How's that?"

"OK. It's what I said but tidied up and put into smoother English. Some of the words don't sound like me. And the bit about moral intelligence. I didn't say that."

"Yes, you did, only not in those words, exactly."

"No. They're your words."

"But they say what you mean, don't they?"

"Yes."

"And you can use them yourself now?"

"I suppose."

"So now they're yours as well as mine."

"Are they?"

"You said Fiorella is a strawberry blonde?"

"What's that got to do with it?"

"Did you make it up? Strawberry blonde. Are they your words?"

"No. My mother said that's what she is."

"But you said them to me as if they were yours. You didn't say they are your mother's, did you?"

"No. But . . ."

"And you joked that white always makes the first move. Did you make that up?"

"No! It's a chess rule."

"Which you were taught when you were learning chess. What I'm trying to say is that we've learned everything we say from something or someone else. You've heard of Oscar Wilde?"

"Didn't he write a story called 'The Selfish Giant' or something?"

"He did."

"My dad read it to me when I was little."

"A playwright. Very witty. One day he heard someone make an especially clever joke, and Wilde said to a friend, 'I wish I'd said that.' To which his friend replied, 'You will, Oscar, you will.'"

He laughed. "But I still say 'moral intelligence' isn't the way I talk."

"Well, it is now, Karl, it is now."

"OK, OK! I give in!"

We laughed, and fell suddenly silent, as if somehow it wasn't so funny after all. And I could see from his eyes he'd had enough of me for the day. I'd had enough of me too.

I waved the printout at him.

"You're giving it to Fiorella?"

"Might as well."

"And not give her the first one about answering the questions?"

"No. It's not right and doesn't matter now I've got this one."

"Want to go on with this or not?"

"Yes."

"Any idea when?"

He pondered for a while, eyes on his feet, which I was beginning to know was a habit with him when he was thinking.

"I'm tied up all next week," he said as he folded the printout and put it into the back pocket of his jeans. "Fiorella is away this weekend on a school trip. I thought I'd go trout fishing. There's a stretch of the Wye that's good for trout. I thought I'd try it on Sunday. Trouble is, it'll take most of the day just to get there."

"The Wye isn't that far, surely? An hour's drive, an hour and a half."

"Too far to cycle and have much time there. And with public transport on a Sunday, train and bus, then a bit of a walk, not to mention getting back . . ."

He wasn't hinting, just making a statement of fact.

Now it was my turn to ponder. I knew that if we were to go on meeting, it shouldn't always be at my place. Too restricting and a bit too formal. He was a guest, on his best behaviour. Besides I needed a change, wanted to get out, have some company, and not with old friends who knew me so well the conversation would be predictable and on a topic I wanted to avoid, but with someone who didn't know me and was refreshing.

But how to make a suggestion without having to explain this?

I decided to take a chance and hoped it wouldn't backfire.

By then Karl was ready to go.

"Look," I said. "I had an attack of sciatica recently."

"My boss had that last year. Off work for a few weeks. Very painful, he said."

"Very. I'm on the mend, but it still hurts to drive. I'm OK as a passenger. But driving any distance isn't on. You're a learner driver, I think you said, and must need to practise, so why don't we take my car, you driving?"

"Do you fish?"

"No."

"Won't you be bored? When I'm fishing, I forget the time."

"I'll read. Take a walk. And I like just sitting and looking at the view."

"I don't know."

"You'd be doing me a favour."

"Ah . . . I get it. One good turn."

"Quid pro quo."

"OK. If you're certain."

"I'm certain."

"What if the weather's bad? I'll still fish."

"So the weather's bad."

"You can't drive to the river. You have to walk down some pretty steep tracks through the woods."

"Walking is good for sciatica."

He gave me one of his assessing looks.

I said, "Range Rover Sports SE."

That clinched it.

"Cool! But only if I pay for the petrol."

"Agreed. Think you can handle the Rover?"

"No problem. I'm good at the practical. It's the theory I fail."

"OK," I said. "I'll bring the food. A deal?"

"See you Sunday."

"Would eight o'clock be too early?"

"Earlier if you like. I'm always on the go by seven."

"Seven thirty?"

"I'll be ready."

# FOUR

------

KARL HAD PRINTED OUT FROM THE INTERNET A SET OF LARGE-scale maps, marking with highlighter our journey to the spot on the Wye where he wanted to fish.

Meticulous, neat, well prepared, the pages inserted into the transparent envelopes of a presentation book.

After the maps, a few pages on rainbow trout, the geography, geology and history of the river.

A man after my own heart: preparation, order and information. The job neatly laid out before setting to.

Karl gave me a quick smile:

"Something for you to read if you get bored."

"Good of you to think of it."

"Well, if you don't fish . . . And it's an all-day job."

"I've brought my laptop."

"You're writing a book?"

I wasn't, but didn't want to explain why.

"There's some eBooks on it. I'll not be bored."

"And if it rains?"

"I'll go back to the car."

We drove through Gloucester, over the Severn, and on towards Ross-on-Wye. In silence. Which suited me, as I'm never talkative early in the day, and Karl seemed content to concentrate on his driving, getting used to the Rover, judging speed and distance still not second nature. But I felt safe, the way you do instantly with some drivers, even when they're learning.

It was also a pleasure to be a passenger, able to shift about in my seat to ease the sciatica, and look at the countryside.

Sunday morning early. Very little moving on the road once we were away from the city.

I could sense Karl settling in, and driving with increasing confidence. Loving the car, its power and strength and robust sleekness.

"You said you'd failed the theory part of the driving test?"

"Four times."

"But you don't have to write anything, do you? Isn't it all multiple choice questions or ticks in boxes?"

"There's more to it than that. Didn't score enough marks. So I was failed."

"There was none of that stuff when I did my test. But that was fifty years ago! And you can't take the practical test on the road till you've passed the theory?"

"Right."

"Aren't there theory tests on the internet for practice?"

"Yes."

"Don't you do them?"

"No."

"Why not?"

"Bloody-mindedness."

"What?"

"It's stupid. I don't do them because I know I can pass the test. The trouble is I go to pieces when I know it's a test. I hate tests. I always fail. So I don't do the practice tests because I know I'd pass them easy. They're not a proper test. And the examiner isn't breathing down my neck."

I knew exactly what he meant because I was the same.

I didn't pursue the topic. The irritation in his voice was a warning, and I didn't want to spoil the pleasure of the day.

Silence again for a few miles before Karl said:

"Can I ask you something?"

"Sure."

"You said you've been married over forty years."

I said, "That's right." Adding quickly to avoid more questions, "Did you give Fiorella the letter we wrote?"

He nodded, eyes firmly on the road.

"And?"

"She asked why I wrote about rugby first."

"And you said?"

"Easiest to start with."

"Have you decided what to write about next?"

"I haven't. But Fiorella has."

"Which is?"

"Love."

*"Love!"*

"She wants to know what I think love is."

I couldn't help a burst of laughter.

"Sorry! But she certainly goes for the jugular."

Now Karl laughed.

"What are you going to say?"

"Dunno. Googled it to find out."

This time I managed to keep a straight face.

"Any use?"

"Pages of the stuff. Loads of sections with titles like 'personal love,' and 'interpersonal love,' and 'cultural views,' and 'religious views,' and 'how to love.' It even had one called 'warnings.'"

"Warnings like what?"

"You must love yourself before you can love another. There's always a risk of getting hurt. Don't ask for love and don't force love, and—"

But he couldn't go on because by now we were both bubbling with laughter.

I managed to say, "Not much help, then?"

"About the same as for plumbing a loo."

"How d'you mean?"

"Easier to find out how to do it by doing it than by reading the manual. Every job is different. The instructions are too general. They don't allow for the quirks."

When we'd calmed down, I said, "Must have been a bit of help, though."

"Nar! I mean, I already knew love is supposed to be like it said. A strong emotion. Feeling attached to somebody. Wanting to be with them all the time. But the bit I liked best was where it said it's impossible to define love because it takes so many forms and is so complicated."

"Like plumbing a loo."

"Exactly."

"But," I said, "when you think of all the books there are on the subject, and the thousands, probably millions, of stories there are about love, you'd think we would know everything there is to know."

"Can't say I've read that many."

"No, but still, the fact is, at least this is how it seems to me, everybody has to learn about it from scratch for themselves. And we all make the same mistakes time and again while we're learning."

"Like me learning to read."

"But not when you were learning to plumb a loo."

"No, I was pretty good at that from the off."

"Every man to his last."

"His what?"

"His own trade. The thing he's best at."

"Like you're best at writing?"

"I'm glad you think so."

"Not that I've read anything you've written."

"And I haven't had the pleasure of your plumbing my loo."

"Anytime. You only have to ask."

"Thank you, good sir. Same goes for my books and you reading them."

"One day, one day. Promise."

"And by the way," I said, "as we're talking about plumbing, could you pull over somewhere suitable, at your earliest convenience. My old man's plumbing isn't as efficient as it used to be and my morning coffee is on the way out."

He smiled and after half a mile or so pulled into a lay-by.

There'd been rain in the night. The hedgerow behind which I relieved myself smelt of rotting vegetation and the spoor left by other travellers observing the calls of nature.

When we were on our way again, I said, "What would you like to do about the letter on love to Fiorella? Would you like me to draft something while you're fishing?"

Karl didn't reply at once, then said, "I've been thinking. I know I asked you for help. But it's a bit of a cop-out for me, isn't it?"

I kept quiet, waiting for him to go on.

Which he did after an uncomfortable silence. "Anyway, what I've done is I've written, I mean I've tried to write, well, I have, I've written, it's only a few lines, a try at it, about love, because I think I should give it a go."

"Great!" I said. "That's great, Karl! And you'll send it?"

He glanced at me, the car wobbled, he attended to his driving again, and said, "Yes, but I thought you might have a look at it while I'm fishing, and, you know, tidy it up a bit maybe, or make a few suggestions."

"Be glad to."

"We're nearly there."

"Not far off," I said, checking the map. "Listen to what Mr. William Wordsworth wrote about the place many years ago:

> *And again I hear*
> *These waters, rolling from their mountain-springs*
> *With a soft inland murmur. Once again*
> *Do I behold these steep and lofty cliffs,*
> *That on a wild secluded scene impress*
> *Thoughts of more deep seclusion . . .*
> *O sylvan Wye! thou wanderer thro' the woods*
> *How oft my spirit has turned to thee!"*

"Sounds like he liked it," Karl said.

"He did."

"And sounds like you like that stuff."

"Poetry? I do."

"Don't know how you remember it."

"The same way you remember how to plumb a bathroom, I suppose."

"Like you said, every man to his trade."

"What I said was, every man to his last. I took my metaphor from the cobblers."

"And it sounds like a load of old cobblers to me."

"Could be," I said.

"Only kidding," he said.

"Me too," I said.

"Fiorella writes poetry."

"Really?"

"I could show you some if you like. I've no idea if it's any good."

"Everybody has to start somewhere. You should see my stuff when I was her age. Embarrassing!" I said, and, checking the map again, added, "Take the second to the right and go straight on to the next lay-by."

# Five

-------

I

How we dote on gear.

The clothes, the gadgets, the tools of our chosen pleasures.

With many people, perhaps most, all this clobber appeals because of our obsession with fashionable regalia.

I sometimes wonder whether most people choose their hobbies because they lust after the gear more than for the benefits of the activities themselves.

Togged up for fishing, Karl didn't just look the part, he *was* the part. And he was so adept with his rod and line it was hard to imagine him ever being a learn-er. While he was fishing, he was a man at home with himself.

I noticed his fishing togs and his gear were well used, and

not only well used but old-fashioned. Perhaps he couldn't afford new stuff and had bought it all secondhand?

‖

You want to know about love what I think about it but I don't know about it not like you mean. I Googled it and it said there are a lot of kinds of love and I think you only mean what people call true love which I don't think is such a good word because love can only be true because if its not its not love is it. anyway all I can tell you is I like being with you and think about you all the time— well not all the time, you cant think about anyone all the time can you because you have to think of other things like when I'm at work if I don't think about what I'm doing I can make mistakes which can be very serious like the other day when I was NOT thinking about what I was doing because I was thinking about you and I forgot to tighten up a clamp on a joint and there was a leak when we turned the water on again and there would have been a flood if I hadn't been there to turn it off and tighten up the clamp. what I mean is I do think about you a lot and want to be with you, I won't say all the time because no one wants to be with the same person all the time do they— be honest but I want to be with you more than

I want to be with any one else, you interest me more than any one else and make me laugh and say things I haven't thought like that before which are important points about love I think and also other important points are respect and admiration which both of which I have for you but what I think you want me to say is that I am in love with you which you say you are with me but this is what I don't know about, well not yet even if I think I am because I don't have anything to compare it with in my life, I mean I haven't been in love before so how do you know

III

Because the early spring day was too cold to sit for long, I read Karl's letter, then took a walk along the riverbank, content in that beautiful place, one of the best in England, to watch some mallards, gem-bright in their mating colours, and let my mind wander along its own track, remembering my wife, Jane, and thinking how much she would have loved it here, until the sun burnt off the overcast, and warmed the day with a foretaste of summer.

I kept well away from Karl so as not to disturb him or the fish. But by midday, having had breakfast so early and the crystal air and exercise giving me an appetite, my stomach was grumbling for lack of its mid-morning coffee and wanting its lunch earlier than usual.

I set up a couple of fold-up camp stools in the dapple of sun and shade between two trees in sight of Karl, who was up to his thighs in the river, laid out the picnic on a fallen tree trunk, and hoped Karl might notice and join me.

I'm sure he'd have gone on fishing all day without a break, lost in the rhythm of casting and dancing his barbed fly on the frobbling water as he wound it in, if he hadn't moved a few metres downstream and was so intent on the spot he was aiming to land his fly he hadn't noticed an overhanging tree, which was in the direct path of the flight of his line. When he whipped it behind him before casting it forward, the hooked fly snagged a branch, and Karl found he'd caught a tree instead of a fish.

As he waded out of the river to disentangle his line, he looked sheepishly around, and saw me watching, unable to keep a grin off my face. For a second he was torn between anger and embarrassed laughter, and, choosing laughter, he shrugged his shoulders, retrieved his fly, rewound his line and joined me.

Then without a word, he set to on the food. I'd made a mix of sandwiches: egg, bacon and tomato; ham, cheese and pickle; cucumber and avocado; chicken, onion and stuffing. He went through half a dozen before I'd finished two.

I learned that day the one-track-minded intensity of Karl's concentration. He didn't like doing more than one thing at a time. And once involved, he'd stick at it for hours.

I also learned, as I'll describe in a minute, the power of some emotions he kept locked away, because he knew that if he let them loose they'd undo his self-control.

"Good nosh," he said when he'd taken the edge off his appetite. "Thanks."

"You're welcome," I said. "Have as much as you want. By the way, I've read your letter."

"Pretty bad, isn't it?" he said, biting into a ham-and-cheese sandwich. "Rammed it down and didn't read it afterwards."

"It's not that bad. I like its honesty. Just needs a bit of tidying up. Shall I do it for you?"

"Please."

"One point, as you mention points."

"What?"

"Do you think you're in love with Fiorella or not?"

"Like I said, I don't know."

"But would you say you've felt stronger and stronger about her since you first met?"

He stopped chewing and thought a moment.

"Yes, I have," he said, took an egg sandwich and started eating again.

"So you could honestly say you love her, and love her more and more?"

He nodded. "I suppose so, yes."

"Maybe you should tell her that? It would help her understand what you feel about her, and it seems to me that's really what she wants to know."

More thinking without chewing.

"That would be OK, yes."

"Would it help if I added a couple of sentences saying that?"

"OK."

He finished off the sandwiches and drank a can of Coke.

I knew him well enough already to sense when he'd had enough of a topic that cut too close to the bone.

I asked, to change the subject, "Caught much?"

"Not too bad. Five."

"Taking them home to eat?"

"See what there is at the end of the day. Pick a couple of the best and put the rest back."

"They're in a keep net?"

"Would you like some?"

"One would be nice, thanks. Very fond of trout."

"How d'you do it?"

"Filleted. White wine. Seasoning. Twenty minutes in the oven."

"Never done it like that."

"Very easy. Very tasty."

"I'll give it a go."

"You certainly have plenty of gear."

He nodded and launched into a mini lecture, showing me each piece as he talked about it. He was, he told me, a Hardy fan—which meant nothing to me. An old firm, I gathered, much admired for their quality. His rod was a Hardy Demon, thirteen foot long, three sections that pulled apart. He described what he liked about it and one or two features he didn't like. His reel was a Cascapedia. (I thought he'd meant Cassiopeia, but on repeating it, as you do when someone uses a word new to you, like a child learning to speak, I was firmly corrected, the syllables of the word clearly enunciated—Cas-ca-pe-di-a.) Its characteristics were itemised and demonstrated. I asked about the flies he used. He opened a little metal box full of them, each fly resting in its own compartment on a bed of cotton wool. They were beautiful little works of representational art, each one different in shape and colours. They had names as alluring as their appearance. I remember March Brown, Morning Glory, Wickham's Fancy, Red Tag and Pheasant Tail. Karl talked about when he'd use them, in which conditions. He handled them with the delicacy of a lepidopterist holding a live and fragile butterfly.

What struck me most as he talked was how fluent he was. Not a hint of hesitation, no stumbling over words or thoughts, his explanations clear and the information well ordered. Just as when fishing he was so absorbed in what he was saying, and in showing me the gear was so full of quiet unselfconscious enthusiasm, that he infected me with his fascination and pleasure. This was a mature and confident Karl, different from the uneasy and sometimes awkward boy who balked at saying anything about himself, who tripped and stumbled when he did, and who couldn't write a reasonably competent sentence.

I watched and listened with admiration. Had Fiorella

seen him like this? If she had, it was obvious why she wanted him, despite his hang-ups and his difference from herself.

Finally he paused and, re-collecting himself, gave me a smile, shrugged and said, "Sorry. Didn't mean to go on like that."

"Not a bit. I enjoyed it," I said. "I can see you like your fishing."

"I do," he said.

"What's the best thing about it?"

He replied without a second's thought, "I forget myself."

"You mean, all your worries, that sort of thing?"

"No. I mean me. Myself."

"Why do you like forgetting yourself?"

"Dunno. Just do."

His shifty look gave him away. He knew all right, but didn't want to explain.

Time to change the subject again.

I thought a moment before saying, "Fiorella wants to know what you believe. Quite a few of her questions are on that topic, aren't they?"

"Yes. But I don't know."

"Well, for a start, do you believe in God? Any god?"

"No."

"What, then? I'm sure you've thought about it."

"I have. And if I hadn't, Fiorella would have made me."

"Does she believe in God?"

"Yes."

"She's Christian and goes to church?"

"No."

"What then?"

"She says she's working it out for herself."

"And wants you to do it with her?"

"Yes."

"So what did you tell her?"

He looked towards the river, wanting, I think, to get back to his fishing, and said with strained tolerance, "What is, is."

"What is, is?"

"What is, is."

"Meaning?"

He glanced at me warily. He really wasn't comfortable with this kind of talk.

"What is there, is there. The river is there. The trees are there. You are there."

I thought for a moment.

I said, "You remind me of a saying by an old Chinese or Japanese philosopher, I forget which. He said, 'When I was young, I thought a river was a river and a mountain was a mountain. When I grew up, I thought a river wasn't a river and a mountain wasn't a mountain. Now I am old, I think a river is a river and a mountain is a mountain.'"

Karl laughed. "I like that. I wish I'd said it."

Laughing too, I said, "You will, Karl, you will."

He laughed again, and took another sandwich and started eating hungrily again.

I was beginning to know him. That movement meant *Enough of this.*

"Well, anyway," I said, "I'm no expert, but it seems to me you're a pretty good fisherman."

"Except when I'm catching trees instead of fish."

Again we laughed.

"How did you get to be so good?" I said. "Did you teach yourself?"

He looked away.

"No . . . My dad."

There was a sudden brittle silence.

Why? Something to do with his father, obviously, but what?

Everything about him at that moment warned me not to ask.

I got out the flask of coffee. Asked him if he'd like some. He said nothing. Head still turned away. No movement.

I filled two mugs and held one out to him.

He took it without looking at me and drank.

Nothing more was said.

When he'd finished his coffee, he stood up and gathered his gear, still avoiding me.

"Thanks," he said and paused on the brink of saying something more, but all that came out was, "See you later."

And he strode off to the river.

A raw nerve touched and no recovery.

Dear Fiorella [or whatever],

You asked me to tell you about love and what I think about it. The trouble is, I don't know quite what I think about it, because I don't know a lot about it. Or at least not like I think you mean.

Don't laugh, but I Googled it. There're pages about it. A lot about different kinds of love. I won't bore you by reporting on all of it.

I think what you mean and want me to tell you about is what people call true love. I don't actually think "true love" is such a good term because love can only be true. If it isn't true it can't be love.

Am I in "true love" with you? All I can tell you is I want to be with you more than I want to be with anyone else. You interest me more than anyone else. You make me laugh and you say things I haven't thought before. These are important points about love, I think, don't you?

Other important points are respect and admiration. I respect and admire you.

But what I think you want me to say more than anything is that I am in love with you, which you say you are with me. But I have to be honest and say I don't know. Well, not yet, even if I think I am, which I do. What makes it difficult for me is that I don't have any previous experience to go on. I have nothing to compare what I feel for you with what I've felt for anyone.

I know some people talk about love at first sight. But I've heard other people say they fell in love gradually. I can tell you that my feelings for you have grown stronger the more I've got to know you. And I want to go on getting to know you more and more. I would call what I feel for you love.

This is the best I can say at present.

*With love* [?], Karl

V

For the next hour or so I rewrote Karl's letter, and took another stroll along the river.

When I got back, Karl was sitting on the bank, his rod by his side, hunched over, his head in his hands.

For a moment I thought he was resting. But no. Instinctively, I felt he was brooding on whatever had upset him earlier.

I debated whether to leave him alone or to make sure he was all right and sit with him for a while. I decided it was better to make sure he was all right, even if it proved a wrong move.

Karl didn't stir when I sat down beside him.

We were silent for some minutes before he raised his

head and clasped his hands in front of him, his elbows resting on his knees.

A few more minutes went by in silence.

Then he took a deep breath, let it out.

"My dad died when I was twelve."

He didn't wait for me to say anything.

"I know it's a long time ago," he went on. "You'd think I'd be over it by now."

I heard him swallow hard.

"I lied to you," he continued when he had gained control again. "I have been here before. Quite a few times . . . It was my dad's favourite place . . ."

Another stumble. Another swallow before he could go on.

"I wanted to prove to myself it was OK, I'd be able to fish here again . . . Remember him . . . Us fishing together."

This time he stopped because he wanted to, not because of a surge of emotion.

"I was all right this morning. It was good. I felt he was with me. Like he always was, standing beside me, telling me where to cast and how to do it better . . . But when you asked about learning . . ."

A long silence.

A flash of shining blue along the river in front of us.

Karl pointed.

"See it?"

"Yes."

"Kingfisher."

"Oh yes! I've never seen one before. Beautiful."

He smiled his pleasure.

I said, "Why come back today especially?"

The smile vanished but he kept my eyes, and with self-defensive sharpness said, "Because today is the sixth anniversary."

"I see. So it's a commemoration as well as a challenge?"

He nodded and turned away.

I needed to move. Sciatica and old man's bones didn't like squatting on the damp, cold ground for long. But something else. Something worse. Jane.

I stood up.

"Maybe you should do something."

"What d'you mean?"

I could tell from the way he said it that he knew what I was getting at.

It seems to me there are two kinds of people. There are those who prefer everything to be spelt out, clear and direct, nothing left to doubt. The others are people who prefer to read between the lines, who don't want every *i* to be dotted, every *t* to be crossed. They need room to decide for themselves what you mean.

I have to confess that by nature I belong to the spellers-out. But I was learning that Karl belonged to the understaters, the ambiguists.

Sometimes the spellers-out need to restrain themselves, and sometimes the understaters need to be given a hint, a clue to help them.

I said, "Maybe you should do something to mark the day."

Karl stood up. We faced the river, side by side.

"Like what?" he said.

"I don't know. Something that would mean something to you. Something that would have meant something to your father."

He thought for a moment before saying with that defensive sharpness of tone again, "You mean something that will help me say good-bye?"

I didn't reply.

"That's what my mother keeps telling me. Let him go, she says."

"Maybe she's right."

"She's always right. That's the trouble."

"And you'd rather she wasn't."

He chuckled. "No." Looked serious again and said, "But I don't want to say good-bye. My dad was the best person in my life."

And he walked away.

Just as well. We were getting into deep water for him and for me, and I knew I'd be out of my depth.

Also I needed to visit a convenient clump of bushes.

VI

When I came back, I said, "Had enough? Ready for home?"

"You said about doing something."

"Yes?"

"Dad always did something. When he'd finished for the day. He always did the same thing."

"Yes?"

"He'd find a bit of stick. He'd cut notches on it, one for each of the fish he'd caught. Then he'd pack up to go. And the last thing he'd do was stand on the bank, say some words, always the same words, then throw the stick into the river."

"He did that every time?"

"Every time."

"A kind of ritual. Did you ask him about it?"

"My dad didn't talk much."

"Like father, like son," I said, smiling.

Karl returned the smile. "I'm a chatterbox compared to him."

"So you never asked?"

"I did once."

"What did he say?"

"'Never take anything for granted.'"

"'Never take anything for granted'? That was all?"

"Yes."

I thought for a bit.

"When I asked you what you believed, you said, 'What is, is.' Did you get that from your dad?"

He nodded and said, "I've found a stick."

He showed me an ash twig about an inch thick and a foot long.

"I've caught five today. I'll make five notches. Then I'll do what Dad did. Want to do it with me?"

We went to the edge of the bank.

Karl sat and cut five snicks through the thin bark, till the white of the wood showed through.

Then he stood up facing the river, me beside him.

He held the stick out in front of him, and in a voice only just loud enough to hear, intoned,

"Water brought thee.
Water take thee.
I have caught thee.
I shall eat thee.
Dwell in me,
As I in thee.
I give thanks
For water,
And for thee."

He dropped the stick into the river.

We watched it swirl away.

# SIX

------

FOR TWO WEEKS AFTER THE FISHING TRIP I HEARD NOTHING from Karl.

Had I upset him? Was he sorry he'd told me about his father? Did he wish he hadn't shared the ritual at the end?

Every day I checked my emails, hoping to see his name, and kept my mobile phone beside me in case he sent a text.

I was surprised at myself. Yet not surprised. I knew he was helping me as much as I hoped I could help him, though he didn't know how, and I still wasn't certain myself.

In the few days after our trip I boned up on dyslexia, wanting to learn more than the sketchy general knowledge I already had.

I can't think without making notes, so I listed what I found out:

*—Dyslexia takes many forms.*

*—There's no one condition you can call dyslexia.*

*—There isn't even agreement on what the word means, except that it comes from an old Greek word meaning "difficulty with words and language."*

*—People with dyslexia usually have trouble with spelling, sometimes reverse numbers and letters—confusing* d *and* b, *for example—and have difficulty with cursive (joined up) writing.*

*—They have difficulty putting their thoughts down on paper—writing is often torture to them.*

*—They are often slow readers, and often need to read the same passage two or three times before they can understand it.*

*—They often mix up left and right, sometimes have difficulty finding their way around, even in familiar surroundings.*

*—They sometimes have difficulty finding the correct word, so they say "whatyoucallit" and "thingies," and get ordinary words twisted.*

*—Their vocabulary is often limited. They don't know as many words as they should. They suffer from verbal poverty.*

*—Because they have had difficulty with reading and writing, they feel they are failures, suffer from low self-esteem and embarrassment, and think they must be stupid. This is often reinforced by the way people treat them, especially if teachers do not understand their condition. Therefore they lack self-confidence.*

It was obvious that Karl suffered from some of these symptoms. Even though he'd only shown me printouts of his writing, when he must have used the spell-checker, I could tell he'd struggled when composing sentences and ordering his thoughts.

But when he talked about something that really interested him, like fishing or plumbing, he was fluent and mature and entirely coherent. You'd never have known he had trouble with words. His vocabulary was far from limited. I knew from his driving that he had no trouble with left and right or finding his way. As a plumber his hand-eye coordination must be good, as I knew it was from watching him fish. Yes, he didn't like talking about his feelings, but many people don't who are not dyslexic.

There was a plethora of guff on the internet about dyslexia, thousands of references. But as usual, finding clear and brief answers to straightforward and simple questions wasn't so easy.

What was certain, which I had already thought for myself but which the experts confirmed, was how best you can help someone who is dyslexic.

They all mentioned the frustration sufferers feel when they are clever, as Karl certainly was, but can't be clever in reading and writing.

Their difficulties are caused by a difference in their brain and the way it works, not because they are lazy or stupid.

They need to be sure you won't make fun of their difficulties, or do anything that makes them look silly in front of others.

Most of all, you need to give them confidence, and to

know, really *know*, that they aren't odd or stupid or have a weird illness.

What they have is different from most people, but is not a disability. In fact, because of their difficulty with language their brains open up new pathways that the brains of the rest of us don't. And those pathways often enable them to be more creative than people who aren't dyslexic.

I was sympathetic with Karl because I'd had trouble with reading and writing when I was a kid. Bad spelling, a slow reader. In fact, couldn't read at all till I was eight. In those days, ordinary people, including teachers, had never heard of dyslexia. So teachers especially thought you were "dull," "not very clever," "thick." "He's a little slow" was how a teacher expressed it to my worried mother. She meant I was halfway to being the village idiot. Not so, as it turned out. I don't blame her. She didn't know better. But that didn't prevent me feeling I was a dead loss, a failure at the two things everybody knows are the most important in our word-dominated society: being able to read and write well.

But something bothered me. Yes, it was true that he showed some of the signs of dyslexia, but not to a serious extreme. And, yes, he was finding ways of dealing with the difficulties—his brain must be opening up the new pathways. And, yes, the last thing you'd say about him was that he was slow-witted. Quite the opposite. He was clever, thoughtful and creative. But I sensed it wasn't only dyslexia that troubled him. It wasn't dyslexia that was jamming up his feelings about himself. And it wasn't dyslexia that prevented him talking about himself. As a recovered dyslexic, I know that I've never been shy of talking about myself and my deepest feelings—so long as it was to someone I liked and trusted.

Of course, he might not want to talk about himself because he was happier keeping himself to himself.

But that's not what I sensed with Karl. I became convinced he was bottling up a brew of strong feelings that he wanted to let out but couldn't. There'd been three or four times when I felt he might explode. And one moment when he had. The moment by the river when he talked about the death of his father. Then I'd caught a glimpse of his inner self. And he was no longer an eighteen-year-old young man, expert at fishing, competent as a plumber, no doubt tough on the rugby field, and good at chess—the young man Fiorella had no doubt fallen for. But instead, he was a little boy, a distressed twelve-year-old, vulnerable, hurt, and grieving.

Hang on, though, I told myself. You could be wrong. It's always a mistake to think you know what makes someone tick.

Karl was right. Actions speak louder than words. When all is said and done, you can only go by what people do, not by what they say.

Now, two weeks after the revelation of his father's death, I'd heard nothing from him. This action, this silence, meant more than words.

But then, just when I'd decided he wanted nothing more to do with me, his name popped up on my screen.
His email's subject line said:

Fiorellas poem

His message read:

Fiorella sent me this poem, is it any good, don't know much about poems, hope you ok, meet tuesday 8?

Not shut out after all!
One of my weaknesses is always to fear the worst. And another is to think that anything that goes wrong is my fault.
I replied:

Tuesday. 8:00 p.m. Meal at the pub? My treat.

He replied pronto:

ok but on me

Here's the poem:

*Two poems for Karl*

1

Do you believe—
As I believe—
What there is
Is all there is?

Do you believe—
As I believe—
That we are
More than we
Yet know?

Do you believe—
As I believe—
You are
Who I would know
And I am
Who you would know
So you can be
What you are
And I can be
What I am?

2

I would be known
As known as
Knowing can be
By you
Who knows
How knowing is
That knows
No knowing.

And I would know
As known as
Knowing can be
The you
Who keeps me
From knowing
The you
Who knows
No knowing.

# seven

- - - - - - -

"IS IT ANY GOOD?" KARL ASKED WHEN WE WERE SETTLED TO
steak and chips (him), sausage and mash (me), a pint of
Brothwaite's Best Brew (him), a glass of red wine (me).

"It's clever."

"Does 'clever' mean good with poems?"

"Not necessarily."

"So what does?"

"Why ask me?"

"You're the expert."

"Me?"

"You're a writer."

"I write stories, not poems."

"So? It's all words, isn't it?"

"Does being an expert plumber make you an expert
gastroenterologist?"

"A what?"

"Gastroenterologist. An expert on your guts."

"What's that got to do with it?"

"They're both experts with pipes."

"D'you have to talk about that when we're eating?"

"You're finicky, then?"

"Only on Tuesdays. So you don't know if Fiorella's poem is any good?"

"Good is a dodgy word when it comes to poetry. To anything actually."

"You're as bad as a politician. Can't you give a straight answer to a simple question?"

"The trouble is it's not a simple question. Nothing is when it comes to poetry. But to satisfy your hunger for my inexpert opinion, I'll admit that her poem may be too clever for its own good."

"You mean she's up her bum?"

"I thought you didn't like that sort of talk on Tuesdays?"

"But is she?"

"I wouldn't put it that way. What I mean is, Fiorella is clearly a clever girl, clever with words. And like a lot of clever people, when they try to write poetry, they think it has to be clever-clever to prove how clever they are. And because they tend to read clever-clever poets they copy them. Well, sometimes they pull it off and sometimes they don't."

"And you think Fiorella hasn't?"

"She has and she hasn't."

"There you go again! Look, if somebody asks me whether a bit of plumbing is any good, I can tell them how

63

well the pipes are fitted and how good the joints are and that sort of stuff. You're a writer. Why can't you tell me how well Fiorella has done her poetry plumbing?"

"All right."

I pushed away my plate of half-eaten sausage and mash, took a printout of Fiorella's poem from my pocket and laid it on the table between us.

"This repetition," I said, "'Do you believe as I believe.' That's all very neat, and she's making a nice point of connecting what you believe, which she must have got from you, and you telling her about yourself. Or rather, not telling her about yourself, which is implied not said."

"And that's good?"

"It's not bad. If she'd left it at that, you could give her, let's say, six out of ten."

"Now you're sounding like a teacher as well as a politician."

"The second part of the poem, the stuff about know and knowing, now that's over the top, in my inexpert opinion."

"Like, you mean if it was plumbing there'd be too many unnecessary pipes and joints?"

"Something like that. Listen, I'll read it to you. That's the best test of poetry: How does it sound?"

"Like does the water run smoothly through the pipes?"

"Exactly."

I read the second part of the poem aloud.

"Oooo! Get her!" hooted a shaven-headed, beer-gutted character of the hot metal variety sitting at the next table. "Poncing with the pooerterwy!"

What followed took my breath away.

Karl turned his head to the intruder, gave him what my mother used to call "a look that could kill," and in a voice of quiet and controlled violence said, "This is the polite version: Mind your own frigging business."

Pause. Tense silence.

Nothing was forthcoming from our gutsy neighbour. He tried to return Karl's uncompromising glare but wasn't up to the confrontation.

His pals sniggered.

Karl waited a further freezing moment before turning back to me, gave me a smile as fresh as spring, and said, "I see what you mean. It's a bit like chewing string."

And he went into an exaggerated riff, over-pronouncing with a po-faced expression and in a voice that mimicked a pompous preacher, the words "Known knowing who knowing knows no knowing who knows you knowing but who knows knowing no knowing but knowing knows knowing when knowing is known . . ."

The effect of which, after the drama of the belligerent neighbour, reduced me to overcompensating laughter, and Karl too when he stopped his blether.


But this was not the end of it. Unfortunately, I was not witness to the debacle.

When we'd run out of laughter and generally calmed down, I said, "Really, we're mean, taking the mickey out of Fiorella's poem. We ought to be ashamed."

"Why?" Karl said. "She's not here. What she doesn't *know*—" Repeating that word almost undid us again, but I held up a warning finger and swallowed the rising chortle.

"Well," Karl continued, also suppressing the urge, "it can't hurt her, can it? And, anyway, even if she was here, it'd be a pretty bad job if she couldn't laugh at herself. I wouldn't want a girlfriend who can't laugh at herself."

"There is that," I said. "Take your work seriously, but don't take yourself too seriously, you mean?"

"Something like that."

"But the thing is," I went on, "what Fiorella doesn't understand is that some people aren't word people like she is."

"What are they, then?"

"They do things. They have to do something before they can say what they mean."

"And you're saying I'm like that?"

"Aren't you?"

Reluctantly: "Maybe."

"Anyway," I said, taking the hint not to pursue the idea. "Fiorella wants a reply, doesn't she? She wants to know what you think. You can hardly tell her you think she's disappearing up her own fundament, now can you?"

"No. But what can I say? I mean, that's honest and not bullshit?"

"Putting myself in her shoes—"

"I'm not sure I want to picture that."

"What helps me as a writer when I ask someone to tell

66

me what they thought of something I've just written—when it's still raw, I mean, and so am I—is that they tell me which bits they liked. That's encouraging, and gives me confidence. And we all need encouragement. As you," I added, looking him seriously in the eyes, "ought to know."

His face blanked. He nodded and looked at the table.

I pushed the printout in front of Karl, stood up and said, "While I visit the wailing wall, take another gander at Fiorella's poem, and see if there's anything you can say you genuinely like. A word, a phrase, a line, a stanza. Anything will do. Then we'll compose a suitable critique."

And I went off to the men's.

While I was there, I heard a sudden rowdy noise followed by a thud like a sack of potatoes hitting the floor. But I was enjoying so much the pleasure of relief—a slow process for men of my age who are suffering the symptoms of trouble with the "waterworks"—and was thinking at the same time about what Karl might write to Fiorella, that I paid only quarter ear attention to the bangarang going on outside.

But when I'd washed my hands, checked myself in the mirror and left the loo, Tom, the publican, who I knew well, was waiting for me in the passage. And he was not happy.

"That young guy who's with you."

His tone as well as his looks indicated trouble.

"Karl? What about him?"

"There's been a bit of a fracas."

"A fracas?"

"I'm not sure what happened, but from what I can gather, him and one of the fellers at the next table got across each other and your guy ended up flooring the other one."

"What? Karl? Never!"

"I didn't see it, so I don't know the ins and outs."

"I can't believe Karl is to blame, even if he did it. He's not the sort to pick a fight."

"I don't care who's to blame. I can't allow that sort of behaviour. Bad for business."

"Where is he now?"

"I turfed the lot of them out and told them not to come back. They're barred. Your lad's outside. The other one was carted off by his pals."

Gobsmacked is the pub word for how I felt. And a sense of guilt that in some way it was my fault.

"I'm sorry," I said. "I'd better—" And made a move to leave.

"The bill," the publican said.

In my confusion I thought he was referring to the police.

"Is that necessary?"

He had the grace to laugh. "The meal?"

What he meant seeped through.

"Oh! Yes, sorry. Look, I'll come back as soon as I've checked on Karl, OK?"

Tom nodded and shrugged.

"You're a good neighbour," he said. "No hard feelings. It's on the house."

I didn't even think to thank him.


It was dusk. Cold and damp.

Karl was sitting, hunched over one of the picnic tables on the pub terrace. No one else around.

I sat down opposite him. But now the sparky, funny young man I'd eaten with had disappeared leaving behind a wary, morose, locked-up teenager almost literally shrunk into himself, who wouldn't or couldn't look me in the eye.

I waited for him to say something. But nothing.

The cold was already getting to me. I wasn't dressed for outside.

"Fancy a cup of coffee?" I said, hoping we might go home where we could at least be warm while Karl gloomed.

He shook his head.

Impasse.

"Look," I said as light-toned as I could manage when my patience weakened. "I don't know what happened. If you don't want to tell me, that's OK. But I would like to know if you're all right."

He nodded.

"You're not hurt?"

He shook his head.

Pause.

But the cold was slicing my bones.

"Well," I said, "if it's OK with you I'll say good night and push off home."

No response.

I stood up. Was about to leave when: "He said something I didn't like."

I waited for more. None was offered.

"What was it?" I asked.

"Doesn't matter."

"It mattered enough for you to have a go at him, if what the publican says is true."

"It was about us."

"Ah!"

"But I didn't do anything then. Only told him to shut it. But the others egged him on."

"So?"

"He stood up and when I wouldn't, he said something worse than before."

"And this time?"

Really, with Karl in this mood it was like extracting teeth with a pair of tweezers.

"I stood up."

"And what then? All of this must have happened pretty quickly. I wasn't in the loo *that* long."

"It did."

"So what happened?"

"He said something else. Punched me in the chest. I gave him a chop and he went down."

"A *chop?* What kind of a chop?"

"Instinctive."

"Where did you hit him?"

"The throat. Side of my hand."

"And that knocked him out?"

"Not exactly."

"What, then?"

"He started choking."

I couldn't help smiling.

"But he's all right?"

"He'll live."

"Let's hope so. And let's hope he doesn't bring charges."

"He won't."

"How can you be so sure?"

"Pride."

"Meaning?"

"Last thing he wants is for it to get round that some little poofter dropped him."

"That's what he called you?"

He nodded. "And me?"

"Yes."

"And that's what riled you?"

"No."

"What did, then?"

"Nasty-minded bigot."

I took a deep breath and paused for thought.

We'd both had enough for that night. We both needed to recover. It was only now, when I knew what had happened,

that my mind caught up with my feelings and needed time
to sort them out and get back into balance. I guessed the
same was true for Karl. And both of us would do best on
our own. But how to part without hurting his feelings or
appearing to desert him when he was clearly in bad shape?

It was Karl who decided, thank goodness.

"I'd better be off," he said. "I'm sorry. I messed up."

I wanted to let him know I didn't mind. "Sure you
wouldn't like a coffee and talk a bit more?"

"Thanks, but I've caused enough trouble for one night."

"You didn't cause the trouble. He did."

"No. Well."

"We still have to decide what you'll say about Fiorella's
poem."

"I'll be in touch. OK?"

"OK. Good night, then."

"See you," he said and fetched his bike.


As I watched him pedal away, I wondered what it was
like to be Karl Williamson. What was it like to live inside his
head? What did he think and feel, awake and asleep? Who
was he? Did he know himself? If he did, he certainly wasn't
letting on. Tonight I'd seen two Karls, almost extremes of
each other, like two hemispheres of himself.

But then, I said to myself, don't I have within me more
than one self? I've seen two Karls tonight, but I've been
two of myself as well. We've both been our summer selves,
bright and confident and warm, and our winter selves,

distressed and dark and cold.

And anyway, who knows all of me? No one. How can anyone know me, when I've spent more than seventy years trying to work out who I am and still don't know all of the answer. Why should Karl know who he was when he'd had much less time to work it out?

# EIGHT

---

I HAD A BAD NIGHT AFTER THE INCIDENT IN THE PUB.

I was worried about Karl. We'd parted on an awkward note. How would he be feeling? I hadn't handled things well.

My impulse was to get in touch. But I'd made a rule from the beginning never to take the initiative but always to wait for Karl to make the next move.

The young are only interested in themselves, and least of all in old people. The old are there to help them. Once the young have what they want, they forget you. I don't ' ' them. I was just the same. We're made that way.

But sometimes you do have to take the initiativ do have to make a move. There are times when the know better. I wondered whether this was such an sion, but decided against it. If Karl needed me, he'd know.

74

Patience. The virtue we need most in old age.

But something else kept me awake. My prostate trouble. Maybe the upset in the pub and my worries afterwards made it worse. Tension, stress, does make many ailments worse, and causes some. Whether the upset caused it or not, that night it was so bad even the strongest analgesics I had in the house didn't dull the pain enough to let me sleep. Up till now it had been worse sometimes more than others, and sometimes it was hardly noticeable. But on the whole it was getting worse all the time.

ere's nothing like pain for turning you in on yourself. orning I wasn't thinking about Karl. My anxiety d entirely on the prospect of an operation and my of hospitals. How much I hate those places! But ot only turns you in on yourself, it reaches a point you'd do anything to get rid of it. So I made an ntment to see the doctor. I'd been putting this off in esperate hope that the trouble might cure itself. But kicked in, and I knew the sooner the condition was with the better.

mention this only because eventually it had reper- ons with Karl.

ate that evening, when I was checking my emails for ast time before going to bed, Karl's name appeared on the screen with the following message:

I dictating this on voice recognition program called Dragon. They gave it to me when they were trying to help me at school with my dyslexia, I thought I'd use it now because it might help me to say what I want to say about fur ellas poem because I can do it better dictating than buy typing it though when I was trying to use this machine in the past. It made as many mistakes as when I do it typing. But I don't have to think about spelling or punctuation, if it gets them wrong that is fault not mine and also I forget most of the commands you have to use. I expect there will be even more mistakes but I'm not going to read this because if I do I probably wouldn't send it. So I'm sorry if there are a lot of mistakes

What I want to say to fur ella is I don't know much about poetry so I'm not the right person to ask about it. I do quite like her poem and I think I see what she's getting at which is just another way of saying she wants to know all the stuff about me that I can't tell her, it's just I don't really know what to say, I mean, if you ask me about fishing or rugby or chess. I would know what to say. I can only talk about things that I know about and things that I believe in, yes, please, I'll have a cup, damn, sorry it will have written that down. It was my mum asking if I want a cup of coffee put off going to bed and spent an hour drafting what I'd come to think of as "a Fiorella letter" and sent it.

In a covering note, I said:

Seems to me your own typing plus spell-check is a lot better than what Dragon does for you.

Yes, I was upset after the pub, but only because I knew you were. Not your fault. There have been times in my life I've walked away when, looking back, I think it would have been better to stand my ground. But at the time it's hard to know which is best or the right thing to do. I agree, letting the other guy call the shots when the shots are violent, even if you can't avoid it, leaves you feeling the loser. Whatever you do and whatever the outcome, you feel you've let yourself down.

Write it off to experience, which is the name, Oscar Wilde said, we give to our mistakes. Besides, the man who never made a mistake never made anything, as Napoleon is supposed to have said, and he ought to know, he made plenty.

How's the following for Fiorella, who I'm amused to see your Dragon calls fur ella.

Hi, Fiorella [or whatever],

I've read your poem and thought about it a lot. I don't know anything about poetry. I don't read much of it—well, none, to tell the truth—and

I don't know what is supposed to make a po
good. But I can see your poem is clever. I m
the way you use language, like the way you pla
the word "know" and "knowing." It also made
think. I can see your poem is really another
of telling me you want to know all about me,
that love is about knowing all about the pe
you love, and the person you love knowir
about you.

You're probably right. But it isn't easy fo
I'm not sure why. The trouble is, it's hard to
down the answers to what you want to
And telling you is hard as well, but not as
as writing. But I haven't told you because v
never alone together for long enough for me
relaxed the way I need to be to talk about m

Also, it seems to me some people are
people, like you, and some are not, like me.
like me need to do something before we
you what we want to say. We are action pe

I've thought about this a lot because
poem, so it has worked like you wanted a
because I have a suggestion.

As I say above, we need to be togeth
enough on our own for me to get into t
mood to tell you what you want to know.

My suggestion is that we go away for t
of your half-term holiday to a nice spot

the country by a river. We could camp there.
ould fish (which helps me to relax a lot). You
uld read and write (or I could teach you to fish!).
u could read me your poetry and explain about
We could play chess.
Have you camped before? (See, there are things
ill don't know about *you*!) I like it and am pretty
 d at it. I've got all the gear—big tent, sleeping
s, etc. I like cooking, as you know. You won't
e to do any of that, if you don't want to. I will
:amp manager, chief cook and bottle washer.
)oing that would be poetry to me.
Vhat do you think?

arl must have gone to bed late as well, because
morning when I booted up, an email from him
waiting, received at 1:33 a.m.

l, thanks. have sent. lot of work next 2 weeks,
time as well, wont see you for a bit, will let
know about camping, hope you ok, karl

# NINE

-------

ABOUT A WEEK LATER, AN EMAIL FROM KARL. FIORELLA HAD
agreed to go camping with him.

Followed by two months without a word.

As I expected, I thought. The camping holiday has
worked out as he hoped. Now he doesn't need my help
anymore.

For me those two months were an uneasy time. The
doctor sent me to a consultant. He arranged tests. The tests
proved the specialist's diagnosis. Prostate trouble, but no
cancer.

With my ready agreement, they prescribed a new drug,
still in the testing stage, which might clear up the problem
without surgery. Anything to avoid hospital.

It took three or four weeks for them to get the strength

e drug right, and for me to get over the side effects
e of which I'd rather forget than describe), but after
here was noticeable improvement. I slept at night,
need to go to the loo so often.

t I didn't forget Karl, thought of him often, wondered
1e was up to. Had he passed his driving test? How
e getting on with Fiorella?

en one morning just before lunch, a phone call.
l's mother, Mrs. Williamson, asking if she could
nd see me.
:ourse I said yes, full of curiosity, and also a touch of
ension. She had sounded edgy.

arrived an hour later.
refused anything to eat or drink. We sat down,
:ach other exactly as Karl and I had been the first
e visited, Mrs. Williamson looking awkward and
ortable on the sofa, me in my chair, trying to look
when I wasn't.

/'s Karl?" I asked to get the conversation going.
ave me a wary, inquiring look that reminded me of
But he didn't take after his mother in appearance.
small, slight, probably petite and pretty and
efore middle age filled her out and her hair turned
1, already flecked with grey. Karl was tall, solidly

83

built, dark haired. But they had the same eyes and as we talked I noticed a number of little mannerisms and tricks of speech they shared.

"It's about Karl I'd like to talk to you," she said.

"Is he all right?" I asked, as calmly as I could, for if he was, why would she want to talk to me about him?

"He's not well," she said with defensive hardness.

A twinge of panic in my guts bent me forward with genuine anxiety. "I'm sorry to hear that. What's the matter?"

"Before I tell you," she said, hard still, "could I ask you something first?"

"Of course."

"*Why*," she said with more aggressive emphasis than I think she intended, because she tried to tone it down by repeating the word with less force. "Why are you so interested in my son?"

I sat back and waited a moment while I took in the implication of her question before saying:

"Forgive me for answering your question with a question. I know how irritating that is. But what do you know about Karl and me?"

Now it was her turn to wait. Were we going to play that awkward game "you answer my question before I answer yours"?

But she said, "I know he came to you about writing to Fiorella. But I also know you went fishing together, and you let him drive your car. And I know something happened that upset him the last time he saw you."

84

"...ut you don't know exactly what happened?"

"...He won't tell me."

...as it right, I wondered, to tell Karl's mother about ...hing he didn't want to tell her himself? Besides, ...ecretive by nature. I don't like telling what I know ...one friend to another, or to anyone else. And I ...like people telling other people what they know ...me.

...t Mrs. Williamson had said Karl was ill, and she was ...ious of our friendship. A worried mother defending ...n. She deserved an answer.

...th a reluctance I hoped she heard in my voice ...: "The last time Karl and I met we had a meal in ...cal pub. I went to the loo. While I was there, a ...nouthed man at the next table said some offensive ...to Karl. Karl tried not to get involved, but the ...ouldn't leave off. He had a go at Karl. Karl in- ...ely defended himself and knocked the man down. ...ublican wasn't too pleased and threw them all

...Mrs. Williamson take this in before adding, "Karl ...o blame. But he was very upset. He thought he'd ...d badly."

...shook her head as if trying to clear it of ugly ...s.

...d, "I've not seen Karl since then. He emailed that ...Fiorella were going camping. I haven't heard from ...n."

There was a long silence.

Mrs. Williamson didn't look at me.

I said, "But that doesn't answer your question, does it?"

Now she did look at me, firm eyed. "No."

I said, "You know I'm a writer and that Karl asked me for help because Fiorella has read my books and wrote me a fan letter and told Karl about me."

"Yes, I know that."

"What you probably don't know is that eighteen months before Karl came to see me my wife died."

Mrs. Williamson's face changed. The hardness vanished.

I said hurriedly, "Please don't say anything. Jane's death is the worst thing that's ever happened to me . . . I was devastated . . . Fell into a deep depression. Like being in a very deep dark pit. A living grave . . ."

I stopped. Thank goodness, Mrs. Williamson remained still and silent. One movement, one word would have breached the dam.

I hadn't spoken about this to anyone for months. Why to a stranger?

When I could, I said, "The worst time was the first anniversary. All I wanted was to die."

It was hard to talk. I blew my nose, looked anywhere but at Mrs. Williamson.

Then on again. I had to finish.

"After that, I decided I had to pull myself out of the pit. Had to accept . . . Well. Anyway . . . But the thing is, I couldn't write. I mean, a book. Writing is my life. When

died, I was in the middle of a novel. But afterwards,
med pointless. I couldn't write a word without feeling

lew my nose again.

)nly two things have ever really mattered to me. Our
)gether and writing novels. And it looked like I'd lost
"

topped again.

heard Mrs. Williamson move and breathe out as if
held her breath all the time I was talking.

long silence again.

rs. Williamson must have sensed it was safe to say
thing now. "Could I get you anything? A drink of
?"

hook my head. An interruption would wreck whatever
 she and I were coming to.

ou miss your wife?" Mrs. Williamson said.

)f course. You miss your husband?"

)f course. How do you miss her?"

Vhat do you mean?"

always felt John was in front of me. Leading me. Now
one, it's like I've been abandoned. I'm on my own.
o be honest I feel lost half the time."

see. Odd you should put it like that. I always felt we
ide by side. I'm a bit of a pessimist. Always expect the
. She made me feel the future was possible."

nd you feel you don't have one now?"

one."

"I think I might feel the same if I didn't have Karl. Have you any children?"

I shook my head again, words stymied.

Silence. We both shifted in our seats.

"Then," Mrs. Williamson said, "my Karl came to see you."

"Yes."

I managed to look at her.

Her eyes were full up too.

"Who has become . . . what? Like a son?"

I couldn't help laughing. Which was, as always, a blessed relief.

Looking puzzled, Mrs. Williamson said, "What's funny?"

"I'm sorry," I said. "It isn't like that. Not that I'd mind. I'd be proud to have Karl as a son. We're alike in a lot of ways, and I've come to admire him. But I wouldn't be a good father."

"Why not?"

"Too hung up on my work. It wouldn't be fair."

"So is it that he makes you feel young again?"

Another laugh. "No. I've given up any hope of that. I know I write fiction, but I'm a realist, not a fantasist."

This time Mrs. Williamson laughed as well. There was the delicious feeling of someone warming to you and you to them.

I said, "I know what you were thinking when you arrived. But it isn't that either."

lo. I'm sorry."

'on't be. It was natural. We're conditioned to be

ious these days."

hat's true. So what was it, then?"

rugged and smiled.

u don't know about writers."

ippose I don't. You're the first I've met."

ll, I'm afraid I must tell you that we're all disgrace-

thless."

hless?"

unscrupulous."

gave me that wary look again. "With my son? You

hless and unscrupulous with Karl?"

xplain."

nk you should."

ers. We can be as nice as pie personally. And

7. But the fact is, everything we do, everything

iens to us, everyone we know, well, it's all grist for

Everything is raw material for work. For what we

telling me Karl is only raw material for you?"

o! Karl is Karl. Young. A breath of fresh air. And

help. I'm old. Tired. In need of fresh air. And in

lp."

kind of help?"

me writing again."

w could Karl do that?"

being Karl and asking me to help him. I tried to

put him off. But he was determined. And very quickly that first time, when he explained his difficulties . . ."

I stopped, trying to assess whether she would understand what I was going to tell her.

"Yes?" she said.

I said, "I saw myself in him. He's stronger than I was at his age, but at the same time, he's as vulnerable as I was. And something else. I'm also dyslexic. Not seriously. I didn't know until a few years ago. But when I was a child, and people didn't know about it, I suffered because of it."

Mrs. Williamson gave me a long assessing look, which ended with a smile.

"I think," she said, "I'm beginning to understand."

"That's a relief."

"Helping my son was helping something in yourself?"

"Repairing an injury."

"And helping him to write to Fiorella got you writing again."

"Exactly. And you know, the strange thing is, it's only as I tell you this that I realise it's true."

"And what are you writing?"

"Nothing."

"I'm sorry? If he got you writing again how can you be writing nothing?"

"Well . . . Let's see . . . How can I put this? . . . A book, a novel, for me, always starts very vaguely. Like a cloud in my imagination. It drifts into view for no reason I know of. It's shapeless. Impossible to get hold of. But it's there. I know

ere. Floating about. But I have no idea what it's made
hat it wants to *be*. What it *means*. And over the years
arned that what I have to do is wait. Wait for the
to take shape, become solid, become something I get
f. Then I can try to catch it in words on paper. And
y when I'm doing that, when I'm writing the words
er, that I find out what it *is*, what it *means*, what it's
to say to me."

Williamson thought for a while. "So there's a cloud
imagination, but you haven't started writing the
et?"

rect."

being with Karl made that happen?"

And I'll always be grateful to him."

ought again.

he know?"

e never talked about it."

thinking.

lerstand what you went through when your wife

been through it too. My husband died when Karl

."

v."

rprised her. "You know?"

ld me."

?"

e day we went fishing."

a deep breath and her eyes filled again.

bes that surprise you?"

"He never tells anybody," she said. "He hates talking about it. Even to me."

I waited.

"It explains a lot," Mrs. Williamson said.

"Explains what?"

"When he told you about his father's death, did you tell him about your wife's?"

"No."

"Why not?"

"Because in my experience, when I'm upset, and I tell someone, and they say, 'Oh, I've been through that too' and start telling me about it, I always feel worse. Seems to me when someone tells you about something that's really upsetting them, what they want is for you to listen to their troubles, not talk to them about your own."

"I don't know. I think it's good sometimes."

"Perhaps."

"And you never told him what he was doing for you?"

"No."

"Well, as I say, I think that explains a lot."

"A lot about what?"

"His illness."

I'd forgotten. Talking about myself, answering her question, I'd forgotten. Panic in the guts again.

"What's happened?"

"Fiorella," Mrs. Williamson said.

"What about her?"

"She broke it off."

What! Why?"

He won't say."

Oh Lord! When?"

While they were camping."

But that's weeks ago."

He came home sooner than expected. He looked ful. I asked him what was the matter. He said Fiorella umped him and burst into tears. I haven't seen him ce his father died."

t he wouldn't explain?"

. For a few days he was all right. Or seemed to be. w, of course, but going to work. I thought he'd get But then he suddenly got worse. He was getting his t to go to work one morning and had a sudden panic Shaking all over, struggling for breath, sweating, stand, couldn't even hold a glass of water. Since hasn't been to work. Mostly stays in his room. lk. Eats very little. He's lost a lot of weight. I don't nat he does all day. Stares at the wall or sleeps as far nake out."

doctor?"

of course. He couldn't get any more out of Karl Depression, he says. Because of the breakup."

nat has he done?"

ibed antidepressants. Offered to arrange for Karl ychotherapist, but Karl refuses. I can't get him to nouse. Won't take any exercise. And for someone s him . . ."

"Have you talked to Fiorella?"

"No."

"Wouldn't that be a good idea?"

"I like Fiorella. But to tell the truth, I never thought it would last."

"Why not?"

"They're both very young, young for their years. They'd fallen head over heels, but it was more passion than good sense. I was never sure what she found so attractive in Karl. In most ways they were chalk and cheese. She's a clever girl. Beautiful and talented. I got on well with her. But her parents weren't happy about it. They are very well off. Professional people. Didn't think a plumber was good enough for her."

"How d'you know?"

"Karl told me. And Fiorella used to joke about it. I think she quite enjoyed going against their wishes. Probably the first time she had."

"So it's not just a lovers' tiff?"

"I don't think so."

"No hope of them getting together again?"

"I'm not sure it would be a good thing if they did."

"You must be worried sick."

"I am. I don't know what to do. I'm afraid of what might happen if he goes on like this much longer . . . I'm desperate, to be honest."

By now I was so upset I needed to collect myself, and I could see Mrs. Williamson was on the edge of caving in as well.

ime for that panacea to which the English resort in
 of crisis.

ook," I said as levelly as I could. "How about a cup of
hile we take stock?"

e looked at me with a faint smile and said, "I'd like
Thanks."

 minutes later we were sitting at the kitchen table
 as Karl and I had sat that first time, had even talked
 made the tea about cooking and housekeeping,
nd I had. The relief of distraction. The comfort of
 everyday chores. The consolation of food.

 a silence that meant we were strong enough to
ress again.

, "When you asked to see me, you thought I might
ne way responsible for what's happened?"

ou still think so?"
he way I did."
 some way?"
t know. I don't know what to think now. All I'm
 that you helped Karl with Fiorella. Then she
f. And that made Karl ill."

k a deep breath and let it out in a long sigh.
I'll do whatever I can. But I don't know what to
 you?"

shed her tea. I offered more. She shook her
said, "One thing I've found out today is that

95

Karl talked to you about something he never ever talks to anyone else about. And for the few weeks when he and Fiorella were getting on well, he was the happiest since his father died. Now he's lost Fiorella and isn't seeing you, and he's worse than when his father died."

Easy to see what she was coming to.

"Do you think you could talk to him? He might open up to you."

My turn to take a deep breath.

"I'm not sure he would."

"I think he would. He talked a lot about how you made him think about things he hadn't thought about before. What he called your cool sense of humour. He took to you."

"Well, if you think it'll do any good, I'll try. But how?"

"You say you suffered from depression after your wife died?"

"Melancholia. Yes."

"So you understand how Karl is feeling."

"I do. But won't he think it odd if I suddenly contacted him after all this time?"

"You invent stories. Surely you can think of a convincing reason?"

"Is he writing emails?"

"I don't know. I don't think so. As I say, he doesn't seem to do anything."

"I can't just turn up. He'd be suspicious, wouldn't he?"

"Yes, he would. But there's something else."

What?"

have to go to work every day. His father had his small business. He was an electrical engineer. I did ffice work and the accounts. After John died, I got hing from a life insurance. I have the house, which ned outright. John was determined about that in e business failed. But there was nothing more. So I earn a living. And with Karl not working . . ."

at do you do?"

retary at our local primary school. I took the job the hours were the same as Karl's. I could be at hen he was. He needed a lot of attention. I'm about leaving him on his own all day."

ou asking if I can be with him?"

every day. Not all the time, of course. But maybe d persuade him to go fishing? Or anything that t him out of the house and give him something think about besides whatever is going on in his e moment."

umped to know what to say. So much emotion, oughts, all at once.

it's a lot to ask," Mrs. Williamson said. "But if ?

silence.

I'm not saying I won't," I said. "I will. I'll do all ve never been quick. I'm a tortoise, not a hare. I've written so few books. I need time to work

Mrs. Williamson stood up. "I'm sorry. I understand."

I got up. "Let me brood about it overnight. I'll get in touch tomorrow. How shall I do that? Shall I phone you?"

"On my mobile, please. Karl doesn't answer the phone these days, but he does ask who's called. I think he always hopes it will be Fiorella."

She gave me her number.

I saw her out.

I went back into the kitchen to clear away the tea things, but before I could do it my knees gave way and I slumped into a chair feeling utterly exhausted, and burst into tears.

# Ten

-------

BAD NIGHT. THIS TIME THE KIND I HAVE IN THE MIDDLE
ιg a novel, when I'm stuck. Thinking this way and
ιat happens if . . . ? Supposing that . . . ? And no
ng answers.

to do about Karl?

ɔ make contact without his suspecting contrivance

sion with his mother?

reason for contacting him? Not Fiorella, which

ke matters worse.

? Perhaps, but why? He knew I wasn't a fisherman.

estions tangled in my mind till around five, when

ι. And woke with a jangling start at nine thirty

ɔostman rang the front door bell. I stumbled

bleary and dazed. A book I'd ordered online.

t in going back to bed. A shower revived me.

Breakfast calmed me. And as so often happens, a thirty-minute walk after breakfast clarified my jumbled nighttime thoughts and supplied the missing link.

What had happened during their time together that caused Fiorella to break up with Karl and go home on her own earlier than planned?

Whatever had happened was the cause of Karl's plunge into depression.

But Karl wouldn't tell his mother or the doctor. So why would he tell me?

If I knew what had happened and could think of a way to get in touch without scaring him off, he might open up as he had with me before, and I'd be prepared for what he told me. It's always easier to help someone when you know what is bothering them and have had time to think about it before getting involved.

So knowing what had happened was the key to unlocking Karl's locked-up soul.

The only other person who knew what had happened was Fiorella.

Maybe she would tell.

It was worth a try.

Hi, Fiorella.

I expect you remember our exchange of emails a year or so ago.

Forgive me for writing to you out of the blue,

100

ut there's something important I'd like to ask you.
ould you mind? Email, MSN, phone, as you prefer.

ckily, it was a weekend. Fiorella was at home. She
d by MSN.

Is it about Karl?

How did you know?

about when we went away together?

do you want to know?

having a very bad time, which started after
rip. He won't say what happened. Only that
oke up with him.

y do you want to know?

ther thinks I might be able to help him,
I helped him before.

ow you helped him and I was furious with
I still am a bit.

Why?

Because I believed he wrote those emails but he didn't, you did. You shouldn't have done it. They were private.

He told you, did he, that I only wrote what he told me to write?

Yes. But writing is not just what is said, is it? It is how it is said. He didn't dictate the words to you, did he? They were your words not his. So I wasn't really getting him, was I?

Did Karl explain why he asked me to help?

Yes.

What did he tell you?

That he is dyslexic and was afraid I wouldn't go on with him if I saw his writing.

Did that matter to you?

No. Why should it? If he had told me from the start I would have helped him. Then he would not have needed to ask you.\

you broke it off with him because he involved
e without telling you and you felt you couldn't
ıst him anymore?

. That was not the reason. I was cross with
n and with you and very upset at first. But I
derstood when he explained. And I would have
given him.

why did you break up?

ɔn't want to tell you that. It has nothing to do
h you.

spect that, if it is what you decide. I'm sorry
t I upset you. I did think it was risky. But Karl
; so insistent and so desperate to do what you
ıted him to do that I couldn't say no.

l, alright. But that has nothing to do with
ıking up with him.

is very ill. If you still feel anything for him,
'll want to help him get better. His mother has
:d me to try and help. But if I'm going to, I need
1ow what happened, and only you know that,
·t from Karl, who won't say.

You are being very hard.

It's hard for me too. I feel I am partly to blame.

Let me think about it.

An hour or so later:

OK. But I want to do it properly. I'll send you an attachment later today.

# ELeven
- - - - - - -

*Fiorella's Attachment*

;ure I want to tell you this. I think I might regret
ld my parents what happened, well, almost all that
l, not all, but no one else. I'm only telling you
ou emotionally blackmailed me. Do I still have
ur Karl? Of course I do! And I don't want him
ecause of anything I've done. Also because you
avourite author. You are not now because of the
iich, whatever you say, *were not his*. I still like
; but I don't like you.
. this is what happened.
ed me to go away with him for the week of
oliday so that we could get to know each other
uoted some teacher or other who told him that
y to find out if you really loved someone and

105

could live with her was to go away with her to a remote cottage in bad weather, and if after a few days you didn't mind seeing her in her dirty underwear and looking her worst, you'd know it would be alright. He thought this very funny. But he also believed it, I think.

I was amused but didn't take it seriously. I mean, what sort of girl is going to risk being seen in her dirty knickers when she goes away for the first time with her boyfriend? What off the beam teacher told him this rubbish?

I must admit I'm not that fond of camping. In fact, I'm not all that keen on outdoor activities, full stop. But I put this aside because I wanted to be with Karl for longer than a day on our own, which is all we had had so far. And he was very keen we should camp together, so I did it for him. It crossed my mind to wonder how it would be if ever we set up together, him wanting to camp and fish and play rugby, and me not wanting any of that. But I pushed the thought away.

Anyway, as it happened we had fun and I enjoyed myself.

Until the crisis. I'm quite good at arranging things, I like having everything neat and exactly right, and Karl is the same. Karl isn't one of those boys, men, who have to be in charge all the time and have their way over everything. He takes pride in what he does, he's careful, he's amazing at paring what you need down to the essentials, and packing everything. He knew I'm not an experienced camper (to say the least). He discussed everything with me. And he tried to make sure we took what would make me

ortable, even if he didn't think it essential. The only
we almost had a row about was the books I wanted
e and what Karl called my "stationery"—notebooks,
pencils, etc.—to which I am addicted and without
my life is unliveable. I countered by pointing out the
t of stuff he was taking for fishing. In the end, we
an agreement, both of us cutting down to manage-
ounts for carrying. But one thing I learned from
s how stubborn he can be. I had to be really firm
e agreed.

that we needed to, because my dad drove us to the
were camping. It was where you spent a day with
told me. This also annoyed me when I found out,
didn't till we were there. We could have taken a
stuff, but for Karl, Dad driving us was just luck,
hould only take what we could carry if we had to
erwise, he said, it wasn't camping, it was setting

irned out, it's just as well we did as he wanted.
re lucky with the weather. There were showers in
a couple of times, and a morning of rain. But I
d the showers because they freshened everything.
gh I'm not keen on camping, I have to admit I
e is something relaxing, and romantic as well,
g in a good rainproof tent, and the smell the
out of the earth and the plants, and the feeling
:ure but very close to nature is really beautiful.
the day Karl fished for hours on end. I knew

he had amazing concentration. I'd noticed this when we played chess. But I didn't know he had such stamina as well. Not that this was a problem, because I'm pretty good at concentrating for longish periods myself. I read a lot while he was fishing and also worked on an essay for school.

The first three days were pretty idyllic. One reason Karl said he wanted us to go away together was that he thought he'd be able to tell me all the things I wanted to know about him, because he'd be relaxed, and we'd have time, and he could do it better by telling me than writing it. I didn't remind him of this during those first three days. I thought it would be best to let him settle in and enjoy himself.

Now I have to tell you something I'd rather not, but it's part of what happened. It's about sex. When Karl and I got together both of us had already lost our virginity. But the first times hadn't been satisfactory for either of us. And neither of us had done any more. So we weren't exactly innocent, but we weren't what you'd call experienced either. Really, we learned about it together. What's for sure is we never enjoyed it so much as during those first three days and nights. But love isn't only about someone's sex, is it? There are more important things about a person than that.

So the first three days went by without us talking about Karl. But on the fourth day, because there was rain in the morning, we stayed in the tent and snuggled together and

ided it was a good time to talk about the things I
'd him to tell me.

ked him again why he found it so difficult to write
rs to my questions. I said I'd liked his emails. Why
't he go on writing them.

got all tensed up at that, and sat up.

ed him what was the matter? What had I said that
im?

vouldn't reply. He closed himself off. The sudden
with the way he'd been, from relaxed and loving to
d hard, hurt me and made me nervous.

v before that week he could be moody. Sometimes
l be full of fun and energy and playful and all
At other times he would be quiet and wanted
l and serious. I didn't know why he was like
vas used to it and didn't mind. But this was

:o soothe him. I said whatever it was it didn't
didn't have to talk about those things that day,
want to. But he wouldn't give, wouldn't look at
ant me to hold him. He'd never been like that

now what to do. I felt like crying but made
couldn't stay lying down. I wanted to move
he tent was too small to stand in and the rain
m going out.

'e sat side by side, cross-legged, not looking

After a while he said he hadn't written the emails.

Just like that. No warning. Straight out.

I thought I must have heard wrongly. But he repeated it. "I didn't write the emails."

I said I didn't understand and asked him what he meant.

It was then he told me about coming to see you and how you'd written the emails for him.

It was one of those times when you can't believe what you're hearing. One part of you does, but another part doesn't. You feel confused, half shocked and half numb.

I said something about how could he do that? How could he deceive me like that? But it was as if someone else inside me was saying this.

He kept saying he was sorry, he hadn't meant to deceive me, he'd done it because he was afraid he'd lose me if he didn't write the answers well enough to please me.

I kept repeating how could he do that? Why did he think I'd not like what he'd written?

He didn't say anything about his dyslexia. He'd never mentioned this and he didn't then. If he'd told me I would have understood. Of course I would. But he didn't. And the longer it went on the more upset I became as what he was telling sunk in and all of me, not just a part, was upset so much I couldn't bear it anymore.

I pushed my way out of the tent. I was in floods of tears. I ran from the tent till I was far enough away for Karl not to hear me sobbing. Then I stood and let the rain fall on me, soaking me to the skin.

was so cold it shocked me out of the shock.

ked that it was so cold. I liked that it took the heat
me. I liked that it was fresh. I liked that it wasn't
, just water. Unthinking, unfeeling, impersonal and

n't know how to put this, but it was the first time in
that I'd felt the comforting pleasure of dispassion.
ssion a word?)
ever.
d there till I'd come to my senses.
I went back to the tent.
it seemed stuffy, smelt of our sweaty bodies,
at from the rainy air.
s sitting where I'd left him.
essed, towelled myself, and pulled on some

ng him this time, and said how upset I was by
ld me, and couldn't understand why he'd done
st be something that would explain it.
ssing. It just felt like there must be.
n he told me about being dyslexic. It came out
rts, like someone trying to sick up something
roat.
e how much he hated it, how it didn't matter
aid, experts saying you're gifted with dyslexia
pposed to make you able to think in ways
en't dyslexic can't, how it made you more
all rubbish. All he knew, he said, was that

111

it had caused him trouble all his life. It had stopped him doing as well as he'd wanted to at school.

Once he got going it was like he couldn't stop. It poured out of him without any fits and starts and not even a pause for me to say anything. He told me how they found out that he was dyslexic, and what they did to try and help, and how the other kids treated him, and the whole story up till now. He told me how the only person who understood properly how he felt and who never treated him as odd or different or a worry or like a patient or in any way at all but as himself was his father. Not even his mother, only his father. He said he was getting on well by the time he went to secondary school, because of the support of his father, and how his father had taught him so much and all the things he loved doing, like fishing, chess, rugby, music, handcraft things, even cooking. And how that came to an end when his father died. After that he'd gone back to feeling like he used to. He explained how becoming a plumber had helped because he was good at it and the guy he was apprenticed to, who was his father's best friend, didn't care a toss about the dyslexia. He told me how he felt about me, which I won't repeat here, and how happy he'd been since we got together. Which is why he was worried about my questions and not writing the answers well enough and why he came to you. He said you'd been a bit like his father, you'd treated him as himself and as an equal and that he'd begun to value your friendship, not only because you'd helped him. He'd been happy again, he said, and now he'd wrecked it.

e didn't ask me to forgive him, but I knew that was
he meant. How could I not? I was still upset. But now
innoyed with you, not him. I could see why he'd come
. He was desperate. But you should have known it
ong for him to send emails you'd written. You could
rsuaded him to tell me about the dyslexia.

, anyway. We talked. I told him I understood. And
see what he wanted wasn't words, but for me to
n it was alright between us. So by the end of the
we were making love again.

st of that day we got back to the way we'd been
it better. It was as if an invisible barrier between
en removed. I hadn't realised it had been there.
oth felt completely free with each other in a way
been before.

cleared. The sun came out. We cleaned up, had
to eat. That afternoon we went for a long walk
It was bliss.

got back Karl fished for a couple of hours
and worked on my essay. But I felt so happy,
in love that I couldn't do anything really
Karl standing in the river casting his line. He
le of nice trout that he cooked and we ate for
eal.

at night better than any before.

by Karl at dawn. There was just enough
nto the tent for me to see him. I have to
had woken me each day at that time to

make love, because he liked it best then. Afterwards we'd go to sleep again. I won't say I didn't like it because I did, but for Karl it was a special time and he was always urgent then.

That morning he was more urgent than I'd ever known him to be. He was, I mean he is, very strong. But he was always tender and thoughtful of me. I liked that. But that morning he was, let's say vigorous.

I'm not going to tell you what happened then because it is too private. All I'll say is I panicked. I was so scared I had to get away.

Suddenly it was as if he'd been switched off. He sort of slumped. Almost like he'd been knocked out.

I didn't know what to do. I said his name but he didn't respond. I pulled on my clothes. And sat facing him again.

His eyes were blank.

I said, I can't deal with this. I made some breakfast, trying to act normal, but he wouldn't eat any of it and neither could I. He just sat there like he was paralysed.

I waited for ages. An hour. Two. I don't know. All I know is I got more and more upset and more and more worried, him in the tent, me outside feeling cold and damp and horrible.

And that was it. I felt I couldn't go on. It was too much for me. So I decided to pack up and go.

When I told Karl all he said was, Do whatever you want.

I started putting my things together. Karl got his fishing gear and went off to the river without even saying good-

r anything. I finished packing, cleared up in the tent
ιe cooking things, made everything as tidy as I could.
∶ft.

∶re wasn't a mobile signal where we camped. As soon
∶t one I phoned home. Luckily, Mum was in. She
nd collected me from a pub in the nearest village.

told her and Dad was that it hadn't gone too well,
l I had had a row and I thought it best to break it off.
∶ pleased. He had nothing against Karl personally
ιght I could do a lot better and it was too soon to
ιs with anyone with university coming up.

was more sympathetic. First love, she said, doesn't
∶t, but I'd always remember it with affection. She
bout her first love, and Dad's. That helped. But
rid of the hurt and the confusion. I just couldn't
l why Karl had acted the way he did. But I was
∶assed to tell even my mother about that part.

now why I've told you. And I haven't told you
ιrt. I'm trusting you to keep all this to yourself.
von't let me down this time. Let's say it's my gift
turn for what your books have meant to me.
ι big difference. This isn't like your stories. It
t's fact.

# TWELVE

-------

I DIDN'T THEN AND WON'T NOW INDULGE IN THE POTTED psychology that might explain Karl's behaviour. What I did spend time brooding about was whether in anything Fiorella had told me there was a clue to how I might get in touch with him, but nothing came to mind.

I hate being unable to solve a puzzle. It nags like a persistent pain, disabling any other occupation. I tussled with myself all day. I asked myself what I'd do if this were one of my novels. What would I do at this point to push the plot on? But after trying this idea and that and each time being defeated by crumbling logic, every move lacking truth-to-life conviction, I accepted that this real-life problem couldn't be solved as if it were fiction, because in a novel I'd go back and change the plot so the stalemate would be avoided. But real life evolves its own unpredictable

over which we characters have little control and only
ndsight, if then, discern the reasons and purposes.
ıe plain unwelcome fact is that sometimes life stymies

at day was one of those that seem to pass without the
went to bed in querulous mood and spent another
night.

ight thirty-five the next morning Mrs. Williamson

ranted to know if Karl was with me. He'd been very
night before. After she got up, she went to his room
he was all right, but his bed hadn't been slept in.
vorried that he might do something—
dn't finish the sentence and didn't need to.
if he might have gone to work.
d she'd phoned his boss, but Karl wasn't with
she thought of me.
if Karl had taken anything—money, extra
thing.
he hadn't.
she had called the police.
ıot yet.
d she should.
to cry.
l she was desperate and beginning to panic.
ether it would be any help if I came over.
ıuld I, please.

The police were helpful but not urgent. Hundreds—thousands—of people go missing every year. Most of them turn up somewhere, if not back at home. Some are never heard of again. A few, comparatively, suffer violent ends inflicted on themselves or by others. Karl, they said, was over eighteen, even though by only a few months, and so was legally an adult, responsible for himself. Even if they found him, they had no power to bring him home or even tell his mother where he was unless he wanted them to. If Mrs. Williamson had any evidence that Karl was a risk to himself or the public, or that he was in danger, in which case they would launch an inquiry, the best they could do was put his name on the missing persons list, and if Mrs. Williamson had a recent photo of Karl they'd add that to the file.

This did nothing to calm Mrs. Williamson's nerves. And I must admit I was worried too, though I tried not to show it.

Best to be practical, to do something.

I asked Mrs. Williamson to look again for anything Karl might have taken with him. But she said nothing was missing. His mobile phone was in his room. He never went anywhere without it. His keys and his wallet with money in it were there too. I wondered if he might have gone fishing. But his tackle was where he kept it in the spare bedroom.

Then it occurred to me. Was he on foot or on his bike?

His bike was kept in the garage. It wasn't there.

Irs. Williamson had had no breakfast. I suggested she
omething while we took stock. She wouldn't eat but
: coffee for us, which we drank while talking over the
>ilities.

rl had taken his bike but nothing else, nothing that
ted he had anything in mind—like buying something
ig somewhere for a day out—nothing except going
here farther than even a longish walk. Unless he just
to cycle round for a while. But why? For exercise
ing sedentary for days? A change of scene, when he
)een out for weeks? To meet someone, when he'd
willing to see anyone for months?
>r all of those.

transport himself far enough away to need his
et there quicker than by walking, somewhere he
go for a purpose brewed up by his self-tormenting
lia.

en a clue.

Mrs. Williamson to have another look round
1. This time she noticed that a photo of Karl's
1't on the table he used as a desk, and wasn't
he drawers or anywhere she looked. "I don't
why I didn't notice it was gone before."

ered how, during the worst time of depression
d, I'd thought about suicide. During the hours
: walls I planned where I would do it, and
w, so that there would be as little clearing up

119

to do as possible by whoever found my body. I wrote letters apologising for causing distress.

Even as I planned this, I knew that thoughts of suicide were normal when you were melancholic. What's more, the antidepressants caused this as well.

I also remembered that when I was planning my death, I didn't want to do it at home because it would have seemed a violation. I chose a favourite haunt of ours. Quiet, off the beaten track, a good place to die, while remembering happy times with the person I loved beyond all description.

Not everyone would think like that. But if I was right about Karl, about the causes of his behaviour with Fiorella and his depression, I could imagine he might.

And I knew something else. I'd intended to hold a picture of my wife so that this would be the last thing I'd see while dying.

Was this what Karl meant to do? It did look frighteningly like it.

I mentioned none of this to Mrs. Williamson.


Life is not like a novel, but a novel can be like life. The best ones always are.

And I thought to myself, if I were writing the story of this moment in Karl's life, there was one place he'd go, whether planning to kill himself or only to wallow in his own pain.

It might seem odd to talk of someone wallowing in pain, but I knew from my experience that people obtain a

ıge pleasure from their suffering. In depression, you're
ly aware of every shift and shimmer of your body, every
·r and twinge of your feelings, every twist and turn of
thoughts, every fantasising image conjured by your
ıation. You are all there is. You are all that matters.
e else, nothing else, has any meaning or importance,
ourself. In the deepest depths you are as high as on
ongest narcotics. And you can loll in that solipsistic
ε for days, months, even years, without requiring
le chemicals to keep you there. It's a self-generated,
cted addiction, the cure of which only you can
The cure is called hope.

ined to Mrs. Williamson where I thought Karl
but not why. As the desperate are, she was ready
any hope of relief.
packed the Rover with the things I might
ıade some sandwiches and a flask of coffee, and
including enough fruit and chocolate to last
ırl loves chocolate"), bottles of soft drinks, a
ıs of beer, as well as Karl's medication and a

re she had my mobile number and I hers,
εr that she would call me at once if there was
would her, and after receiving a hug and a
f thanks, drove off at precisely ten o'clock.

# THIRTEEN
-------

HE WAS THERE.

And he was alive.

I stopped, hidden among the trees a hundred metres or so from him. I could hardly stand for relief.

The glade by the river where we'd spent the crisp early spring day, and where he'd camped with Fiorella in the heat of summer, was gemmed in cool golden autumn, the trees moulting their leaves.

I'd parked in the lay-by and walked the ten-minute trek down the wooded valley as quietly as I could. I didn't want him to hear me in case he did something desperate before I could reach him.

My first thought was to let Mrs. Williamson know. But I remembered there wasn't a signal, though I checked to make sure. I didn't want to go back to the road, where there

one, for fear that Karl might do something untoward
...ve before I got back.

...hen I first saw him, he was standing, head down,
...e edge of the riverbank. Was he preparing to throw
...f in? I took off the backpack so I'd be ready to rescue
...ut after a few moments he walked a couple of steps,
...up a rock big enough to need two hands to lift it,
...he carried a few steps from the river to a pile of
...bout knee high. He placed the stone carefully on
...od back and surveyed the pile, then returned to
...and stood again, head down for a few moments,
...cking up another stone from the water's edge and
...it to the pile.

...ack-and-forth business went on long enough to
...pile up to his chest height, forming a roughly
...ramid-like mound, wide at the bottom, tapering
...op. It reminded me of the cairns that mark the
...ints and sacred sites on the Yorkshire moors
...iked in my youth.

...to worry about what I'd do if this went on all
...lready feeling cold—the autumn air among the
...bottom of the valley was chill with damp. My
...ttled ways had been upset by the events of the
...eakfast was four hours ago and I'd not had my
...g coffee because I'd driven nonstop from Karl's
...ing the speed limit wherever I dared, I have to

123

confess). In the backpack were the coffee and sandwiches Mrs. Williamson had made. But they were intended for Karl more than me.

How long had I been hiding here? Going on an hour.

Time to make a move. I'd decompose into compost if I stayed much longer.

Making as if I were just arriving, I broke cover, walked to the river as if unaware of Karl, and sat myself down in a patch of sunlight on the edge of the riverbank ten metres or so from where he was standing, head down, looking into the water.

I opened the backpack, took out the flask and box of sandwiches, poured a mug of coffee, drank it, opened the box, took out a sandwich and began to eat.

It was hard not to glance at Karl, but I managed to keep my eyes to myself.

I took my time with this performance, a spur-of-the-moment, unthought improvisation, inspired by the basic need to eat and drink and warm up. The gentle autumn sun on my face and the refreshing ripple of the river at my feet raised my spirits.

Again I was going on my own experience of melancholia. It had helped to have a sympathetic friend with me, so long as they didn't talk much, and didn't ask about how I was feeling and why and offer suggestions for "getting better." Silent companionship, yes. Fuss and advice, no.

I'd finished one sandwich when Karl came and sat down

e me. I pushed the sandwich box towards him. He took
lwich and began to eat. I poured a mug of coffee and
lown near him. I helped myself to a second sandwich
e it. He too, after drinking his coffee. I refilled both
ugs. When the sandwiches were finished—five for
vo for me—I held the bar of chocolate out to him.
k it and set to work eating it.

died the view—the river dappled and ribbled with
:, the harlequin autumn trees rising up the valley
:.

inished the chocolate.

' did you know?" he said to his feet.

swork," I said to the river. "It's what I'd have

lurking about behind that tree, did you?"

d to myself. "Never much good at the scouting

d.

l away the box and flask.

shing gear is in the car," I said.

ike."

) come with me to get it?"

here."

it you might want to let your mother know you

sandwiches."

but I forgot my mobile."

I do?"

urself."

quick as I can."

125

"No rush."

We looked at each other for the first time.

He gave me a down-turned smile. "I'm not going any-where."

A risk. A test of my trust. And trust dies from ifs and buts.

I was back in thirty minutes. It had taken a ten-minute call to Mrs. Williamson to give her time to vent her relief and to reassure her that Karl was all right, that I'd not leave him, would take care of him whatever happened, and get him home as soon as he'd agree. She wanted to know why he'd left without telling her, and what he was doing. I had to tell her I didn't know and thought it best for Karl to explain when he felt he wanted to, that there was no use questioning him, it would only dam him up and even turn him away. I could hear in her voice as she rang off—"Give him all my love, tell him I'm here for him anytime"—that her relief was tangled with the anxiety of absence.

When I got back, Karl was busy piling more stones onto his cairn. He stopped when I arrived and again we sat side by side contemplating the view, his fishing tackle lying between us.

Coffee is, for the old, a potent diuretic. After twenty minutes or so I had to make for the trees. When I returned, Karl was assembling his rod.

"Anything left in the sandwich box?" he asked.

pened it. He took some cheese, nipped off a small
rubbed it into a ball between his fingers, and threaded
through it on the end of the line.

ot fly-fishing today?"

shook his head.

ill they go for that?"

a good day some coarse fish go for anything. Bread,
meat, cheese. Cupboard bait."

re was a backwater pool under a tree a few metres
arl cast his line into it, and remained sitting, rod in
yes on the float.

ng the next hour or so—for once I didn't check my
he caught nothing, now and then wound in his
ewed the bait, and cast again.

hat was only displacement activity, keeping his
usy while he did something else, something that
tell took all his will power against the resentful
of his melancholia.

he did was talk. Not the fluent flow of the time
ry spot when he told me about his love of fishing,
bs squeezed out of his mouth, expectorations of
d phrases, sometimes a few sentences together. It
ne part of him was trying to speak while the other
to strangle the words before he could say them.

te down what he said in the tormented fashion
t was spoken—I've tried to do it—is as tortuous
it was to hear and for Karl to utter. So instead

127

I've composed his monologue—which it mostly was, because I interrupted only to ask a question now and then—into a continuous speech that accurately honours, I hope, his meaning, and uses his own words as far as I recall them—which isn't difficult because Karl's declaration was so unsparing of himself and so trusting of me that I shall remember it for the rest of my life.

# FOURTeen

- - - - - - -

*Karl's Declaration*

to do it.
e here to do it.
rked out how.
ught about it for days.
s as well.
t sleep much.
d it.
ver and over it in my mind.
want to do it at home because of Mother. Took
I did to decide to do it because of her. Thinking
uld do to her.
ind of built up in me.
re I thought of doing it the harder it got not to
he less I thought of Mother or anybody else.

By the time I decided last night I wasn't thinking about
anybody except myself.

I didn't care about anybody anymore.

I just wanted to end the pain.

*What pain? What caused it?*

Don't know.

Hard to say.

Fiorella.

She dumped me.

And what I did then.

The way I behaved.

That started it.

And Dad.

It brought him back.

Not having him.

Him not being here.

It all got mixed up.

My fault about Fiorella.

Don't know what came over me.

*Why? What did you do?*

Doesn't matter.

It did her in and she dumped me.

And then it all came over me.

Like it had been waiting to happen for ages.

Well—since my dad.

lon't know.

was like sliding down into a deep pit, a deep dark
and I couldn't stop myself. Down and down. Leaving
:hing behind.

:n myself.

e I wasn't me anymore.

e a fish when you've gutted it and what's left when
eaten the good bits. The bones. The carcass.

t like that.

rcass.

still alive.

struggle.

try.

:he longer it went on the harder it got.

I'd been drugged with poison.

:d my energy.

it everything. Even myself.

here wasn't any hope of ever getting any of it back

ven myself.

getting out of the pit.

getting anything right again.

*nt on like this for quite a while, going over and over*
*:lt, as if repeating it was the only way to understand*
*to understand himself. Until finally I said:]*

*lost.*

131

Lost?

Everything lost.

Whatever.

Anyway, it got too much.

Couldn't stand it anymore.

Just wanted it to stop.

That's what happened last night.

Couldn't take it anymore so I came here to do it.

*Why here?*

D'you believe in life after death?

*No.*

No. Nor me neither.

Dad didn't.

He used to say what is *is* and you'll know what is when it happens.

And he said the people who say they know are the worst.

But do you believe anything of you stays behind?

*I don't know.*

Nor me neither.

But I've never felt Dad has gone.

I mean, sometimes I feel if I turn round he'll be there.

1im like he was. I mean, not . . . well . . . flesh and
. But him. Somehow him. Him. There.
ve you ever felt that about somebody?


o?

*wife.*

wife?

*dead.*

1ever said.


dered.
se she was never there when I came to see you and
mentioned her.
1nyway.
ing is, Dad loved this place.
1 the best time here.
1e went I've tried not to think too much about

elp it, though.
eling he was still there, still here somehow. I

133

thought if I came back it might help.

That's why I came here with you.

I didn't want to do it on my own and not with Mother.

And coming here with you and, you know, the thing with the memory stick. It was good. I liked it.

And because there was Fiorella.

And you'd been like—

Well, you'd been a help.

I was feeling so good. Fit and well. Really fit and really well for the first time since Dad went. I thought I must be getting over it, must be accepting it, because I hadn't yet.

I see that now.


*So bringing Fiorella here was a kind of celebration.*


If you want to put it like that.

A celebration of Dad.

And a celebration of Fiorella and me.

I didn't tell her that.

Maybe I should have.

Maybe she'd have understood.

I thought it would be great, really good.

This morning, when a lot of this stuff has come clear, I saw I was kind of bringing Fiorella to meet Dad, to show her off to him.

Does that sound daft?


*No. It sounds true.*

nd it was like that at first.
r three days it was like that.
d nights.
ghts like I'd never imagined nights could be.
never been so happy.
be I was too happy.
you be too happy?
be you can. Maybe when you're too happy you
whatever you want is possible. Everything can be
you want it to be. Nothing can stop you.
what I felt here with Fiorella.
now what I mean?
I'm saying?

*what you mean.*

r had it like that before.
nean just the sex. But, you know, all of it, the
one in the night.
e everything came together then, all of me.
?

ny mind, all my feelings, all my thoughts.

it was the same for her.

I know it was.

She said it was.

And it was when we were together like that is when it happened.

*What? . . .*

*What happened?*

Like a wave.

Like a tidal wave.

Like a tsunami, rushing up like I was a boat on the wave, carried on the wave, not able to stop or change direction.

Not that I wanted to. No no!

It was good, it was so, *so* good!

And while it was happening this stuff started coming out of my mouth.

About having a baby.

About wanting us to have a baby.

About starting it right then . . .

I don't know where it came from.

It was me. But it wasn't me saying it.

I was out of it.

Out of my head.

Out of myself.

I was gone.

But I was all here as well.

All there.

'anting us to have a baby . . .

ried to make her.

ıke her let me . . .

: got scared.

dn't mean to scare her.

she got scared.

made me stop.

then I felt so—

ked.

myself.

dn't speak.

ln't look at her.

ıed.

*ıs panting, almost hyperventilating. Sweat covered*
*lis eyes were big and staring. I felt he was seeing*
*serving himself, as he had been at that moment,*
*ame time he was experiencing it again, and he was*
*himself.*
*ed and said nothing for a while, until the fit had*
*e was calm again.]*

hat was it.

n't take it.

d her.

:d me.

:t her back.

to say sorry and explain.

But she wouldn't talk to me.

Her mother answered.

I don't think she ever liked Fiorella going with me.

I know her father didn't.

She said Fiorella didn't want to speak to me or see me ever again and I should leave her alone.

That's when the slide started.

Couldn't get her out of my mind.

Couldn't give her up.

And that's when I started fretting about Dad again.

And it got so bad I couldn't go to work.

I didn't want to go to work.

I didn't want to do anything or see anybody.

Couldn't leave my room.

I knew I was worrying Mum sick. But it was like I was stuck in mud. All the energy sucked out of me.

I could hardly move.

Spent the day staring at the walls doing nothing, the same thoughts, the same feelings sloshing around inside me like blocked-up plumbing that's gone wrong.

*Maybe it had. Maybe the plumbing in your mind had gone wrong.*

You mean I'd gone crazy?

I tell you, thinking about it now, it does seem like I was crazy.

This morning I feel like I've just come out of the loony

138

t I didn't feel crazy at the time.

e plumbing might be dodgy but not my thoughts.

 body felt pretty grotty, but everything I was thinking

d logical.

ogical as a game of chess, every move planned, and

 clear.

st Dad.

st Fiorella.


*huckled. A bitter sound.*]


ing and the queen both out of the game!

here wasn't a hope in hell of getting them back.

 lost.

o on?

o end it.


*haven't.*


*pped you?*


vas thinking about it.

 hours.

king about how to do it.

 up on the internet.

One site listed all the ways. But it said, if you mess it up, you end up a basket case. A vegetable. Still alive but worse off than before and not able to do anything about it.

For the best ways, the surest ways, I didn't have the gear.

Like a gun or poison that worked in seconds.

But even if I had, nothing like that seemed right.

I wanted to do it somehow that seemed right.

Does this sound silly?

I mean, it's like choosing the right fishing gear, or a car, or, I dunno, anything. You want what suits you.

Well, it was like that.

Another site had examples of the way some famous people had done it.

And there was one, a famous writer, the way she did it I knew was the right way for me.

Everything sort of came together then.

I knew the place, and the place had what I needed for the way I wanted to do it.


*I think I know the writer who you mean. Water and stones.*


I love water. Always have. Dad too. He taught me to swim when I was a baby. So young I don't even remember.

But if I chucked myself into the river I wouldn't be able to stop myself from swimming.

So I was going to fill my backpack with heavy stones, and tie some to my hands and feet.

*The pile on the bank.*

at's how it started.

*t there's a lot more than you'd need.*

*smiled. A first since I'd arrived. But still didn't look at*

*come?*

s dawn when I got here.

gh light to see by.

d looking for stones.

had to be right as well.

y right.

shape. Right look.

ou noticed the stones in the water by the bank?

s and shapes and colours.

vater they look so bright. So fresh.

ms.

ht it would be easy to find what I wanted.

asn't.

first one on the bank.

next.

other.

ing because I kept thinking I might find one

he others.

ot to be like I couldn't stop.

It was like when I'm fishing.

You know?

*Concentrated, absorbed, you forget everything. Time. Other people.*

The pile got higher and higher.

And then it got so big it got top heavy and fell over.

Collapsed.

I didn't like that.

It was a mess.

I hate messes.

So I started again.

But this time I kind of planned it.

Made a square of bigger stones, bigger than I'd need except for the base.

When I'd laid the base, like a platform, I had a thought.

I'd brought a photo of Dad to have with me when I did it.

But now I thought I'd bury it in the pile of stones.

*A memorial.*

Sort of.

Yes. A memorial.

I think I still meant to do it.

But I wanted to build this memorial to Dad and him

me being here.

his time it took a lot longer than before.

r each layer I had to have the right size and shape of

, getting smaller towards the top, to make the thing

nd stable.

eded a lot more stones as well.

kept going.

you know what?

?

d to enjoy it.

e more I went on, the better I wanted it to be,

tter I made it, the more I enjoyed it.

ndoing what I'd done and redoing it better.

tter stones from the river for each layer.

's when you turned up.

*led again. Smiled again. Looked at me.*]

*the trees.*

are no good at!

*how relieved I was when I saw you.*

ed when I saw you.

I was still going to do it.

But then I saw you.

And I wasn't.


[*He turned away.*

*Stood up.*

*Took up his rod, which he'd laid down on the ground before he started his declaration, and wound in the line.*

*Nothing on the hook. Not even the bait.*

*He chuckled again at this.*

*I waited for him to say some more. There was so much more I wanted to know.*

*But he said nothing and I sensed he'd said all he was going to say today.*]


[*I stood up.*

*He put his hand into a pocket, took it out, turned to me, holding out his hand, which was clasping something.*

*He waited a moment, then opened his hand.*

*Lying in the palm was a small rust-red stone, about the size of my thumbnail.*

*It was smooth and round, with flat sides.*

*And there was a hole through the middle.*

*Like a very small doughnut.*

*I couldn't tell whether it was natural. Or the hole was man-made.*]

For you.

'hy? What is it?

present.
te it.

ok it. It was unexpectedly heavy for its size.]

nk you.

s at a loss for any other words.]

is a hand to finish.

ned away and walked to the stone pile, the memorial.
ted my present and followed him.]

# FIFteen

-------

WE FINISHED BUILDING THE CAIRN WITHOUT MUCH BEING SAID, except of a practical sort—which stones to use; how to construct the cairn so that it was stable and solid—the photo of his father buried at its heart.

Karl was concentrated, as if all the emotions of his declaration were absorbed into the stones and his attention to our work.

By the time we were done the cairn looked sufficiently monumental for anyone who came across it to see it was more than merely a pile of stones. About a metre square at the base, it stood a metre and a half high, tapering to a flat top about thirty centimetres square, which we capped with a slab of slate just the right size that we'd found in the river.

We stood for a moment or two, side by side, looking at it.

elt something should be said to mark the occasion,
ouldn't think of anything appropriate.

en we washed our hands and faces in the river,
ted our belongings, and strolled in single file, Karl
g the way, up to the car. We retrieved Karl's bike from
dge where he'd hidden it and stowed it in the back of
over. And then I phoned Mrs. Williamson to let her
we were on our way.

now I was feeling the pinch. My old man's energy
up to such unrelenting activity and emotional
d downs. And the long drive, without a stop,
e shifting of heavy stones had set off the sciatica.
st thing I felt like doing was drive the car back
I'd supposed Karl would do this, but he climbed
e passenger seat without a word, and by the
phoned his mother and eased into the driver's
was fast asleep, out like a light and dead to the

to stop three times to walk about, rest my back,
ult the hedgerows. Karl never woke, never moved
he entire journey.

we got back, Mrs. Williamson, not knowing
to laugh or cry, did both simultaneously. The
son responded as best he could, but all he wanted
to bed. His mother urged food on him, a bath,
a litany of questions about how he was and what
d ("Just bed, Mum, just bed"), and telling him

how good I'd been and wasn't I clever to know where to find him.

All to no avail. Karl was in bed, unwashed, unfed and unconscious fifteen minutes after we arrived.

As for me, I wanted to be back in my own home and to attend to myself no less than Karl wanted his bed. But out of fellow feeling accepted Mrs. Williamson's offer of a meal while I gave her a brief report on what had happened, including the building of the cairn, but omitting Karl's declaration, which I knew would raise many questions to which I neither knew the answers nor had the stamina to discuss. I left her to nurse her relieved delight on her own as soon as I could, promising to phone later.

I felt a touch guilty, leaving her like that, but there are times when guilt is no rival to the need to save yourself.

When I phoned late that evening, Mrs. Williamson reported that Karl had slept until about six, then got up, showered, ate a meal of fried eggs and bacon, before going back to bed, where he still was, fast asleep. He'd said very little, except that he "felt a bit better" but was "knackered."

We agreed his fatigue was natural and understandable and was perhaps a good sign that he was recovering.

Mrs. Williamson, however, was as lively as a bumblebee, still buzzing with relief, gratitude and maternal desire to coddle her only child.

I promised I'd phone again next morning, which I did,

not till midday. I, too, was knackered. To adapt the
us lines from the Remembrance Day poem, age does
them, and the years do condemn those who live to
. There is no escaping the deracination of time. I felt
n by the previous day's excursions. But the pain of
sciatica prevented solid sleep. My joints ached, my
lt filleted of their bones, and I was urinating even
en than usual and with some pain. No position,
sitting or lying down, was comfortable for long.
hrough this before, much worse, and knew that
vas the only cure for my body and listening to
only salve for my soul. Exhaustion that would
l no more than a good night's sleep for recovery
ears ago, now required three or four.
when I phoned, Mrs. Williamson sounded as
mbled down from yesterday's high and fallen
Karl, however, was up and in better shape
weeks. He was in the garden "pottering
ther said. Of course, he hadn't gone to work,
it, if indeed he was on the mend, which it
n to know. Mrs. Williamson was staying
job, because she was afraid to leave Karl
relapsed." She was worried about being

it, I'd have offered to Karl-sit. But my
ssion were as weak as the rest of me. I
norrow, which seemed to cheer her up.

I phoned early next morning, intending to be at Karl's in time for Mrs. Williamson to go to work as usual. But she said Karl wanted to be on his own, had persuaded her that he would be OK, wouldn't "do anything silly," and needed her to trust he'd "get himself back onto his feet." He had agreed that she could phone him whenever she wanted to. I asked her to tell Karl he could phone or come and see me at any time.

That day passed without a word from Karl. Mrs. Williamson phoned during her lunch break to tell me that Karl was pottering about in the garden, and again when she got home that afternoon, to tell me he was making another fly for his fishing.

Next day, the same calls, and the day after. The fourth day, Mrs. Williamson reported that Karl had cleared his room out and—for the next three days—was repainting it, the walls white, the woodwork the shade of blue, Karl had told his mother, of the song thrush's eggs.

Each day she sounded more cheerful and confident. But "we're not out of the wood yet," she added with a defensive caution against disappointment that I'd come to recognise was part of her nature.

And so as the days went by, I called less and less frequently, and so did Mrs. Williamson. It became clear that Karl was much better and improving in spirits all the time.

though still not going to work, he was keeping himself
at home and had started fishing again in the local

ring that time my doctor arranged for me to see a
tant, who advised I might need a prostate operation
next few months if the medication I was taking
how better results soon. Luckily, the condition was
the early stages and, he suggested, could be dealt
hout too much difficulty, the prognosis being good
nplete recovery.
began to occupy me—by which I mean worry
re than my concern for Karl. Of course, I didn't
t to Mrs. Williamson, though there were moments
d to resist a temptation to spill the beans. One of
ms of living on your own at my age, after more
years of married life, is having no one at home to
ut your worries, no one who can shore up your
and cheer you up. Friends, however good and
ot the same support as a loving partner, who
nside out.

of weeks later Fiorella's name popped up in my

Karl is ill. Is he OK?

had told her.

His boss. He's doing some work in our house. What's wrong with Karl? Is it serious? His boss says it is.

It was. But he's getting better.

What was it?

It's not right for me to tell you.

That means it must be mental or emotional, because if he'd broken a leg or something physical was wrong, I think you'd tell me.

No comment.

Was it because of what happened between us?

No comment.

I bet it was. I wish you'd tell me because if it is I feel I'm to blame. Partly anyway.

I wouldn't say you're to blame.

So it is, isn't it? I'd like to see him.

I thought you'd broken up with him for good.

did, but I can't forget him, can't get him out of
y mind. Maybe what happened wasn't so bad.
frightened me and I panicked. I've thought a lot
out it. I think I can see why he behaved like he
. He was all mixed up about his dad and me and
being able to write like I wanted him to. What
ou think?

't know.

k he needs me. I could help him get better.
want to see him again. I'll try to.

you, of course. But it wouldn't be a good
st to turn up at his house unexpected.

e some credit.

uck.

# sixteen

----- - - -

|

A couple of weeks went by after that without anything more from either Karl or Fiorella.

Mrs. Williamson called every two or three days to keep me up to date—Karl was pretty much the same.

During the third week the good news was that Karl had gone back to work. Only part-time but a good sign. He found the first week hard going but stuck at it. Though he was still morose now and then, his mother felt he was at last on the mend.

Then, the following week, I had a phone call. The organiser of a weekend conference for teachers on the subject of teaching novels. They'd planned a talk by a famous author for Saturday after lunch, but she had cancelled because of

nily crisis, and they wondered if I could "save their
n." A very good fee was offered, all expenses paid, hotel
nmodation if required. I was assured of the delightful
e of the location—a comfortable conference hotel in
evon countryside—and of a hearty welcome from the
ed and fifty appreciative teachers. I suppose on the
rassment-saving principle of "never explain, never
ise," nothing was said about why I hadn't been their
oice, or indeed how many other possible substitutes
pproached before coming to me. But then, I didn't
be told. I have no illusions that I am anything other
author of minor importance, who enjoys, if that is
l, a devoted but small readership.

rst impulse was to refuse. I hate public speaking,
because I'm not very good at it; I detest anything
h selling myself or my books; I dislike socialising
ebrity guest; and, to be frank, felt a bit miffed at
ehorned in as the last-minute replacement for the
g author everybody was expecting to meet.

s impulse was stifled by—what? The seduction
Even as the understudy, at least I'd been invited,
er much you dislike yourself for it, flattery does
e persuasive than that, the prospect of publicity.
o write a book than sell it, as every publisher
tell you if you complain about your poor sales.
us in the word business know that authors
ders is the best way of selling their books. I've
tood why readers are so influenced by meeting

155

writers. As a reader myself, it's the last thing I want to do. In my experience most writers of books you've admired are disappointing as people. How can it be otherwise? If they're any use as writers, the best of them will be in their books.

So, out of vanity and crude commercial judgement, I accepted. As there was no convenient rail service, I said I'd drive there on Saturday morning in time for lunch, and return home after my talk.

I regretted this as soon as I put the phone down. Had to restrain myself from phoning back and cancelling. But no. It would have been unprofessional.

To get me out of the house—an action that would quieten my troubled mind—I drove to the local petrol station and filled up and put the car through the washer— but knew by the time I got home, even from that short trip, I'd be crippled by sciatica after a two-and-a-half-hour drive, never mind the drive back. I could stay overnight to give myself a rest before driving home, but the thought of spending the evening with a crowd of teachers letting their hair down decided me against that solution. And though I could do it all in one day by train, I didn't fancy a long train journey with two changes. Besides, the weather was cold and grey, and all my instincts were urging me to hibernate.

Again I thought of cancelling. But dithered.

Then I thought of Karl. Perhaps he'd drive me. Perhaps he'd like a day out. And one more persuasion. Apparently there was a sculpture park in the extensive grounds of the hotel, which was bounded by a river ng "excellent trout fishing available to hotel guests."

for Karl while I was at the conference—three
ur hours at most, but enough perhaps to tempt

ich it did. We agreed to set off at eight on Saturday
ng. When we got there, Karl would fish while I
d with the teachers, then set off home about four.
y seven, traffic and weather permitting.

‖

the journey neither of us was talkative. I never am
public appearance. My mind is all on what I'm
say. My nerves are agitated by fear of failure. I'm
n and irritable.

as, I guess, regretful, wishing he'd refused. I knew
own time in the pit of depression that you grow
enjoy your illness, even when it's at its worst,
to be shut away on your own, no one else to
but yourself, wallowing in the slough of your
g condition, like a hippopotamus lolling about
slough of mud.

to say, we had to stop after an hour for me to
dge.

got back into the car, instead of driving on,
g ahead as if at something blocking the way,

I me?"

It took a moment to adjust my enclosed mind. "You mean, why are you you rather than someone else?"

"Why am I me? D'you ever wonder why you are you?"

"Doesn't everyone?"

"Do they? Does anyone know why?"

"I very much doubt it."

"You know how many people there are in the world?"

"Billions?"

"Very nearly seven billion. That's seven with nine noughts after it."

"Unimaginable." (And can we please get on?)

"Why am I not one of them and not me? Don't you think it's weird to be you and not someone else?"

"If anything's weird, the weird thing is being human."

A pause. No sign of getting on.

I said, "I thought you believed that what is *is* and that's all there is to it."

"I do normally."

"What do you mean, normally?"

"Before. I'm not normal now, am I? I haven't been normal for ages."

"You mean, since the crisis."

"Yes. When I was really bad, I mean the worst time. I couldn't stand being only me. And not knowing why. I wanted to stop being me. I just wanted to stop. I wanted not to be. I wanted to be nothing."

"And now you're over the worst?"

...nce at the river. Not wanting to get rid of myself. I do
...e what is *is*. Only I keep wanting to know why. And
...  ..."

...hat?"

...vish  ..."

...ish what?"

...on't know. I don't know how to say it. I don't know
... wish or how to say about being me and about why."

... mind was at sixes and sevens now, wanting to say
...ing useful, but mainly wanting to think about
...etched talk, and get there, and get it done, and get
...ome, and so I said nothing, having nothing worth

... waited a moment, before coming to, starting up
...ving on.

... rest of the journey passed with only the occasional
...f talk, about the route, or the weather (fine, cold,
... a couple of showers), or the countryside (winter
...in, the trees waiting for a final stormy blow to shed
...maining leaves).

...pt that out of the blue Karl mentioned receiving an
...om Fiorella, saying she'd heard from his boss he was
...x ill, and asking how he was.

...ed whether he'd replied. He said he hadn't. I didn't

III

I won't describe my reception and performance at the conference. It has nothing to do with Karl. Except to say that afterwards, as usual, I felt a total failure, and suffered minor agonies of embarrassment about what I did say and how I said it, and what I didn't say and how I should have said it. Had I been on my own I'd have driven away at once and spent the journey in recovery by verbally flagellating myself for my ineptitude. But I had to find Karl and shift the gears of my mood from self-abusing sulks to at least a semblance of civility.

I walked down to the river but couldn't find him. No one else was around to ask if they'd seen him. The grounds of the hotel—once a stately home, it was even better than its publicity, a rare quality—were extensive, partly wooded, partly parkland. I didn't fancy trekking everywhere, on the hunt for him. In my disordered state of mind, I began to worry that he might after all have done something silly. I knew how easy it was to slip back into the pit while clawing your way out of it.

What to do?

Calm down, I told myself. Think sensibly.

Of course! Phone him! I took out my mobile and rang his number. Karl answered. Relief!

I said I was ready to go home, where was he? He said he was looking at something he'd like me to see and told me how to find him. He sounded excited, quite the opposite

160

ı his earlier moroseness, and the first time I'd heard
note in his voice since the crisis began.

I've mentioned, the hotel included a "sculpture
—a path that wound through the grounds, with
ıres by many artists displayed here and there.

ı was in a glade in the wooded area, sitting on a
leaning forward, arms on thighs, hands clasped
—a posture I'd learned he adopted when thinking
e was gazing at what looked to me like a pile of
ıngled metal rods perched on top of a block of
e.

n't budge when I sat down beside him, and only
moments of silence said,

l'you think?"

bout?"

ed at the pile of rods.

now. Meant to be a sculpture, obviously."

it's made?"

ls."

ı all one piece, no joins. One length of steel
ent by the same kind of tool we use to make
"

flows quite attractively. Turning in on itself
It looks a bit like a doodle drawn with a

D."

ı doodle."

d walked round the sculpture, running

his hand along the rod, feeling its shape, then standing back to view it, here and there bending down to look at it from below. There was energy in his movements, vigour and concentration.

"It's different from every angle," he said. "You wouldn't think that something so simple could make such different shapes from different angles. And it's so good to look at, you can't help touching it."

He toured twice more before I said, "Maybe the artist—"

"William Tucker," Karl said, pointing to a label on the base. "And it's called *Beulah One.*"

"I wonder what that means."

"No idea."

"Maybe it doesn't mean anything. Maybe it's only meant to be something pleasant to look at."

"You mean, it's just a . . . just a *thing* . . . End of story?"

"Why not? If you want to put it that way."

"A thing that pleased him."

"Like a poem, only made of a steel rod, not words."

Karl looked at me and smiled.

"I like that!" he said. "Poetry in steel. That's good!"

He sat down again.

"I've been looking at it for ages," he said. "And the more I look at it, the more I want to look at it."

We were silent for a while. But, as ever, I was aware of the time and wanted to be home because by now I was feeling cold and damp. If I stay much longer, I thought, I'll come down with a cold or my joints will seize up.

ook," I said, "I hate to be a spoilsport, but I'd rather

 make for home, if you wouldn't mind."

 got up. But his eyes were still on the sculpture. He

 over to it and ran his hand along a curving section

 sorry," I said.

," he said, coming back to me, "it's OK."

 walked to the car and drove away.

ere was another," Karl said, when we'd settled into

rney. "By a different artist. It was made of rods as

hey were shaped into the outline of two people, a

d a woman, very tall, taller than real people. It's like

ere drawn in the air. I saw that one first. Looked at

ges."

 was like a man woken from a long sleep, and

ed by breakfast.

 you do any fishing?" I asked.

. I thought I'd have a walk round, to stretch my legs

e drive, and have some coffee first. I saw some of

lptures, which I quite liked. Hadn't seen anything

m before. Then came across the one of the man

man outlined in steel rods. The others had been all

ut this one really impressed me. And the way it was

f bent rods welded together made me think of my

I sat on a bench near it and had some coffee and, I

ow, went on just sitting there for ages, looking at

pture, and thinking."

"Thinking what?"

"Nothing much."

"But thinking?"

"Not about anything really."

"Thoughtless thinking?"

"Thoughtless thinking?"

He gave me a quick glance, and we both laughed.

"Or maybe," I said, "letting your body do the thinking."

He stared at me, as if in surprise.

"Body thinking?" he said.

And broke into a fit of laughter, as if he had heard the best joke in the world. He was laughing so much he couldn't speak and had to stop the car till the fit wore off, when he said: "Yes. Body thinking. That's what I do."

I waited till he'd calmed down before saying, "And then?"

"Nothing. Sat there for I don't know how long. Meant to go back to the car for my gear, but must have turned the wrong way, because I got a bit lost. And then I came across the sculpture that really grabbed me. The other one was meant to be a man and a woman. But this one wasn't anything except, like you said, just a shape, just a *thing*. As soon as I saw it, I felt . . . well, I felt it was mine . . . That sounds stupid when I say it."

"Not stupid at all. I've felt that about a book. A novel."

"That it was yours? That it had been made only for you?"

"A long time ago. When I was young."

'Well, anyway, I couldn't help it. I just had to sit and
at it."

\nd do some body thinking?"

'ou could say. The others were made of various stuff.

and stone and concrete. But the man and woman

is *Beulah One* were made of nothing except some

ds. They were as simple as you can get. But the

looked at them, the more I got out of them. That's

ked."

bu're glad you came?"

lad I came, thanks. But, hey, I haven't asked how

1. Was it OK?"

aid, soonest forgotten."

as that?"

t bad, not good. But that kind of carry-on isn't

is you?"

paper. Reading them and writing them."

l. "So all you are is words on paper?"

But when I'm on my own, reading and

ost myself and most at home with myself.

y, I see we need some petrol. We'd better

xt service station."

guess is right, you'll need to consult the

to know me too well, young man!"

# seventeen
-------

SOMETIMES I WONDER IF WE REALLY DO BRING UNPLEASANT things upon ourselves just because we say they might happen. Isn't that why we say "touch wood" or "don't speak too soon" or "don't count your chickens before they're hatched"?

Of course, it's all baloney, mere superstition. But still, when I came down with 'flu a couple of days after sitting too long in the cold and damp, I couldn't help thinking that if I hadn't thought of it then, it might never have happened.

Whatever, I woke on Monday morning as floppy as a wet rag, aching in every muscle and joint, sweating as if in a sauna, my nose feeling like it was full of frothy soap, and my eyes streaming.

They say the young have the ability but lack the wisdom, and the old have the wisdom but lack the ability.

rudely true generalisation. That morning the wisdom
xperience told me I had a bad case of the 'flu, but the
lity of old age prevented me from doing much about

ook a couple of analgesic pills, drank some water and
bed bemoaning my bad luck.
on't go on about the following forty-eight hours
they have nothing to do with Karl's story.
next thing that happened, which does, was a phone
Mrs. Williamson on the Thursday evening. (For
o, like myself, keep track of time, this was five
the trip.)
ason she called wasn't mentioned because as soon
d my voice she asked if I was all right. I replied as
lly as I could that I had "a bit of a cold."
und dreadful," she said, which cheered me up

" I said. "I'm fine."
aren't," she said. "How long have you been

nday. But it's nothing to fuss about."
ou picked it up on Saturday, talking to all
ome of them were bound to be full of cold.
it about."
ialogue on such occasions then followed,
errogation into whether I was up or in bed
s looking after me (myself), was I drinking
especially fruit juice (yes: a lie; honest

answer: very little, because I was too weak to bother), what had I eaten (cornflakes, toast and marmalade), how often (enough; untrue: once), what was I taking (analgesics, but I didn't add that I'd run out of them), was there anything I needed?

The last question was the clincher. I did need the pills, I was almost out of milk and cornflakes, and, as she had mentioned it, could do with some orange juice and ice cream. I was at the stage when your mouth is a cesspit and your throat is coated with little shards of spiky glass. Orange juice and ice cream would go down a treat.

So I gave in and asked if she might—if it wasn't too much trouble—and if she had time—buy me the above-mentioned items and bring them for me next morning.

Reply: No trouble. Could she get in without my having to come down to open the door? Answer: How very kind, and if she came to the back door, she'd find the emergency key hidden in a tin under a flower pot, three flower pots to the left of the door.

"Not exactly a big test for an apprentice burglar," Mrs. Williamson said.

My batteries were too low to spark a laugh or a witty retort.

I'd never heard her so chirpy. But I've noticed women quite often get like that when you're under the weather and they take charge. Jane was the same. Perhaps there's

ething in the female genes that releases chirpiness when
maternal impulses are given full rein, not to say, reign.
ad I must say, I was only too happy to be reigned.
are times when coddling is the best medicine.

e it from me, whatever you do, do *not* volunteer to
swelling ranks of the ancientry. Live long enough,
lly-nilly, you'll be conscripted. The benefits are
the perks are few and the future prospects are
tive.
hing to ensure is to keep your mind busy when
ing with things you can keep your mind busy with
re old. Then, if—or rather when—your body lets
you will still have plenty of mental pleasures to
. Of course, if your mind goes before your body,
You won't know anything about it.
there is one benefit of old age that I should
cause for permanent celebration, one distinct
u aren't a teenager anymore, and never will be
fflicted again.
ny consolation for those currently tormented
of adolescence, it will soon end and there's
many years of adult pleasures ahead before
ed into the delights of what people these
cally call "the third age," by which they
increasing decrepitude.
going to say on this tedious topic.

Mrs. Williamson sorted me out, fed and watered me, groomed and refreshed me with such care and attention and so efficiently that I hardly had time to grumble about it.

With me reconditioned, she started on the reason why she had phoned.

"I'm worried about Karl," she said.

Not again! I thought. Not a relapse?

"He's acting very strangely," she continued.

"Why? What's he doing?"

"That's just it. I don't know. He shuts himself up in the garden shed and is there for hours."

"Have you asked him?"

"You know what he's like. You can't get a word out of him when he doesn't want to."

"He must have said something."

"'Just messing about,' he says. 'I'll tell you later,' he says. But he's been at it all week, all the time when he's not at work."

"So he is going to work?"

"Still half-time. To be honest, I think it's time he went full-time. You know him. He has to be busy."

"You haven't looked in the shed when he's out?"

"He keeps it locked. And he blocks the window with a board when he's not there."

"How does he seem? I mean, is he depressed like before, or what?"

"No. He's better than he's been for ages. When he was

170

ie hadn't enough energy to get out of bed. Now he has
e than he knows what to do with."

from one extreme to the other."

xactly."

least he's not mooning about."

ue. Before, he was dying of breath, now he's fit to

couldn't help smiling at each other.

ild you have a word with him?" Mrs. Williamson
ind out what's going on. I don't think you under-
ow fond he is of you and how much he listens

't know about that. Can't think I've said anything
at's worth much."

I know it sounds like sucking up, saying nice
bersuade you, but it's true, whether you know it
tually, I rather like it that you don't know. It's a
y. But, anyway, would you have a try?"

a moment, to be sure, before saying, "To be
se or not, I'm intrigued. What on earth can he

have a word with him?"

n being intrigued, which was a reason I was
lliamson would understand, I have to admit
fond of Karl. I was concerned about him.
was something of the paternal stirring in me
here was something else as well, which I'll
inute.

I said, "Phoning him won't do. He'll clam up. I'll have to see him."

Mrs. Williamson sighed with relief, but instantly looked anxious again.

"But you're not well enough," she said. "You must take care of yourself."

I was pleased she didn't add "at your age," though I suspected that's what she meant.

I was also learning she was a woman who lived on her nerves, sensitive to the smallest changes in the psychic weather. I could only imagine how much she had suffered these last months as her only child was battered and bruised, and what devastation she must have endured after the loss of her husband.

I said, "I'm feeling better already, thanks to you. I'll get up and see how I manage. If I'm OK, how about we fix for me to come to your place tomorrow? That's Saturday. Karl will be home, won't he? But we need a good excuse."

A silence for thought.

Then Mrs. Williamson perked up and said, "How about I invite you to lunch, as a thank-you for helping when Karl . . . had his episode? I think he'd like that, though he'll not admit it."

"Sounds good to me."

"All right. What about lunch tomorrow, so long as you feel up to it?"

"Thank you kindly."

"As you've been very naughty this week and not eaten

172

erly, it'll be best to give you something light. What
t some sea bass gently poached, a few new potatoes
salad? It's a favourite of Karl's, who'll probably do the
ng."

ot on! Looking forward to it already. But let me
ome ice cream for after."

et the impression you're an ice cream junky."

ive to confess a slight addiction."

oth laughed, more heartily than the joke deserved,
deal was done.

Williamson wasn't my only visitor that day. There
her, virtual this time, not visceral. Fiorella in my

Author. I do wish you'd update yourself.
so yesterday. Thought I'd let you know I
today. He was with his boss doing stuff in
s flat. I don't know what you've all been
about. He didn't look one bit ill. In fact,
I in pretty good shape to me. Really, to
I quite fell for him all over again. But
p this to yourself or I'll never forgive
t so far as to invite him for a game of
orrow but he said he was too busy.
AT? I ask you, because he wouldn't tell
n consumed with curiosity. Please tell
you'll know. I asked him about you.

He said you'd been out for a day together. I was somewhat jealous but suppressed this unworthy reaction. Please please PLEASE tell me what he's doing. I promise not to let on to ANYONE, least of all Karl. I mean, I've just trusted you with a secret. You can trust me. I'm really really agog to know. And what do you think? Should I try and get together with him again? Do you think he wants that as well? Do you think what happened when we were away was an aberration? A one-off? Has he said anything about it? He's so lovely. I'd welcome your advice. With love from Fiorella desperado.

It was an email that switched off my reply button. Let it wait.

Had no one taught Ms. Fiorella Seabourne about appropriate register when addressing your elders, or does no one care about such niceties anymore?

But then I thought, it isn't her fault. Why do adults complain when young people do or say things badly, inappropriately, lacking manners, when it's adults who are meant to teach them how to do things properly?

So I relented.

Hi, Fiorella. I am beyond hope of updating.

Am sorry but I don't know what Karl is doing.

As for whether you should try and get together with him again, I'm afraid I am no use as an agony

cle. And I have no idea what he wants. My own
neral approach to such matters is: The nose
ows.

Saluté.

ne more note before I finish this chapter. I mentioned
another reason why I wanted to know what Karl was

I've explained, I hadn't been able to write a book
Jane died. Her death seemed to kill the writer in me.
t all along, since my first meeting with Karl, in the
scious back of my mind—the womb where all
est creative ideas have their conception and their
on—something had been growing. And now, that
ay, as Mrs. Williamson appealed to me, a finger
d out from my unconscious and I knew with sudden
the following:

e recording of Karl's encounters with me and mine
im, our shared experiences, was a story I could write.
s story would not be fiction. It would be a true-life
I didn't have to invent anything. As yet, at that time,
d was unknown. The plot was revealing itself as we
.

alised only then that it was not writing that had died
my wife died, but invention. I had had enough of
ion. The facts of life, life as it is actually lived, was
now mattered to me, all I wanted to think about,
nted to write about. What I had to do was set down

a record of what I knew about Karl and had experienced with him. It would be his story, not my story. And that also pleased me. I had had enough of myself.

Later that day, I settled at my desk for the first time in more than a year to do what I feel I was made to do. I began making the notes, writing down all I remembered of Karl's story so far, ready to begin writing it when I knew the end.

It was, it is, in every sense, a labour of love.

# EIGHteen

- - - - - - -

EMEMBER THAT EXPERIMENT WITH IRON FILINGS AND A
t the science teacher did at school when you were
ge still easy to amaze? You remember the way the
ngs, which were scattered like a mess of dust on a
paper, suddenly formed into clean strong patterns
ne magnet was placed in the middle of the mess,
g the magnet's magnetic field? Oo-arr, from the
o'd never seen this magic before. (Do they still do
chools?)

reminded of this when I arrived at the Williamsons
day and saw Karl preparing lunch. Since the crisis,
een like the mess of iron filings. Disarranged. Now
nagnetised, his filings composed into the pattern
f. It isn't an exaggeration to say he was glowing
gy. The change was palpable. Before, he had been
ith himself. Now he was comfortable in his skin.

Some words from my religious past came to mind. He once was lost, and now is found.


Good spirits are infectious.

Mrs. Williamson was jocular, which I had not seen before. I caught a glimpse of what she must have been like when she was young and happily married, with infant Karl to coddle and tend.

She did a good line in joshing.

"Come and meet the master chef," she said with a wink when she let me in. And teased Karl now and then during the meal, a tickling he enjoyed while pretending poker-faced toleration of his mother's jokes.

Another pretence—that I was there as a thank-you—was kept up throughout the meal. And because nothing could be said about why I was really there, and any talk of recent unhappy events would have dampened the jollity, Mrs. Williamson plumped for the safe strategy of asking me the usual questions people ask a writer. How I got started and why, how many books I'd written and what kind. Which led by association to where I was born, and what my parents did, and what kind of boy I'd been. But no questions about my wife, for which I was grateful.

Karl listened but said nothing. He played the part of cook and waiter with the easy care I'd come to know was natural to him, whatever he did. But at the same time I sensed he'd rather I hadn't been asked about myself, and I wondered why. The clue came later.

By the time we were eating the ice cream I'd brought as
contribution, I was puzzling how to introduce the topic
arl's activity in the shed without spooking him. I knew
baulk, shy away and clam up if I got it wrong. We'd
ied the meal before I'd made up my mind. But need
ave worried. Mrs. Williamson knew her son, and was
d with more savvy than I'd so far guessed at.

ave you noticed," she said to me, still in her joshing
how craftsmen never clear up after themselves? They
bourers to skivvy for them. His father was like that.
te father, like son. So you two go and do whatever
after feeding their faces, while I clear the table and
e dishes."

ot up and began stacking the plates, and as she did
over her son, kissed him on the head, and said in
une voice, "That was a delicious meal, my love.
or making it."

hear!" I said.

fected a suitable modesty, but a blush and lowered
yed his pleasure.

help you," I said, out of politeness, but without
nove, aware of what she was up to.

ou won't, thank you all the same," Mrs.
1 said. "You're a guest, and in this house guests
ores."

off into the kitchen.

at Karl, smiled, and shrugged.

p, nodded "Follow me," and without a word

led the way through the kitchen, out the back door, down a path at the side of the lawn to a substantial shed at the bottom of the garden.

I don't mean to boast when I say I had an inkling of what I would be shown.

The shed was generously kitted out. A multitude of tools and gear neatly arranged, everything in its place. And filled with that workshop smell of sawdust and oil mixed with the tang of electricity given off by power tools. A handyman's paradise.

This was a quick impression, because my eye was caught at once by a number of objects—eight or nine—carefully placed on the workbench, like a little exhibition. They were made of thick black wire bent into a variety of shapes. Some were very simple, no more than two or three separate lengths, bent into shapes and placed together in what was clearly meant to be an intended, not an accidental, arrangement. Others were more complicated, made of one length of wire bent into elaborate, almost knotted inter-windings.

I could see the inspiration for some of them was William Tucker's sculpture, which is what I'd guessed I'd find. Others were quite different.

Words are the worst tools for describing objects. I don't know whether teachers still do it, but when I was a kid, they used to give us an exercise that began with the instruction,

gine that a man from outer space has come to Earth.
ribe a screwdriver to him as clearly as you can."

ie spaceman, poor guy, has presumably wandered up
omehow indicated—because of course he can't speak
arth language—that his UFO has conked out and
ou help him, please. In a flash, without a moment
l on intelligent astonishment, you give him a detailed
rtion of a screwdriver, regardless of the fact that he
understand a word you're saying and assuming
t further investigation that this is the implement the
d spaceman needs.

he pleasures of school, where, we're told, we spend
oiest days of our lives!

enough to describe objects with an everyday
purpose, it's impossible to describe objects that
eant to be used, that don't look like anything
seen before, and are made out of material like
d metal pipes, and pieces of wood and stone and
ptures. Objects made into shapes that represent
ccept the shape itself. And even if they are objects
sent things we know—landscapes, buildings,
ants, animals, the sea, whatever—they aren't
ie described, or presumably their makers would
words rather than made the objects. They are
nded for you to look at and work out what they
the feelings and thoughts they excite in you.
words, works of art.

is, art objects aren't meant to be described. If

there's anything to be said about them it's what you want to say because of what they have done to you.

As I looked at Karl's miniature sculptures I rather dreaded he'd ask me what I thought of them and whether I liked them. I'm not good at instant reactions to anything. I need time to take in what I've experienced before I can say anything intelligent.

I'm sure most people would have asked what I thought. But Karl didn't. Another example of his difference from most people and of his sensitivity. He waited long enough for me to have a good look from various angles before he spoke.

"I know they are bad copies of the one we saw at the hotel."

I said, "Some. Not all. But I wouldn't say bad. And what does it matter if they are? Copies, I mean."

"I wanted them to be a bit different. A bit more . . . my own."

We weren't looking at each other, but at the sculptures.

I said, "When you started as a plumber, didn't your boss show you what to do and how to do it and then you did it the way he showed you?"

"Yes."

"And when your dad taught you to fish, did he show you how and then you did what he did?"

"Yes."

"Isn't that copying?"

suppose."

sn't that how we learn everything? By copying people
know how to do it and show us?"

Iadn't thought of it like that."

iere was a high stool in a corner. I sat on it. Karl
ed himself onto the workbench.

aid, "When I was fifteen, I wasn't regarded as clever,
wasn't much of a reader. But one day I came across a
I started reading just because I had nothing else to do.
: know why I picked it rather than another. Anyway,
ed reading. It didn't hook me straightaway. It didn't
he kind of catchy opening that grabs your attention.
well into it before this strange thing happened that
:ver happened before. I just couldn't stop reading it.
; I read the last page, all I wanted to do was write a
ike that. I wanted it so much, I started straightaway.
iave the story. It's about eighty pages long. Eighty-
be exact. It took me six months. When I read it now,
es me laugh, because it's so obviously a bad copy of
)k I'd read. But it got me going. It showed me what
:d to do with my life. It showed me what *I am*."

: put a silence on both of us.

:n the emotion had drained away, Karl said, "What
aying is something like that has happened to me."

)t my eyes, as I felt his eyes were, too, on his
.gs.

replied, "Hasn't it?"

How hard it is to admit to someone else who has recognised it before you have yourself, that something has happened to you, which will reshape your life. Perhaps because you resent that they have noticed before you have. Perhaps because such an admission reveals your deepest and most vulnerable self. The self we all fear someone will injure or hurt or destroy.

And it's hard because you know at that very moment of recognition that your future is decided. That whatever happens, come what may and whether you want to or not, you will have to live your life in a way determined by your discovery of what you are and what you are meant to be.

At one and the same moment, you suddenly feel free— free to be who you are—and at the same time restricted, bound, unfree, because you can be nothing else. In gaining your freedom to be you have lost your choice of being anything else.

I sensed Karl was struggling with that very dilemma before he answered in a voice forced through a jammed mouth.

"Yes."


After such moments of a truth declared and accepted, discomfort sets in.

What should you do? Break the ice by telling a joke? Change the subject?

I thought of suggesting we leave it there for today, but that felt like dodging the questions still hanging in the air.

All I could do was take the advice I'd given Fiorella:
ow my nose.

I'm guessing these are models," I said. "D'you plan to
e them the right size?"

)ne or two," Karl said. "The ones I'm pleased with."

Vhich are?"

: pointed to two. One very like William Tucker's, the
a more complicated arrangement of entangled and
knotted wires.

d making them out of pipes?"

e Tucker one. But the other one I'd like to make out
less steel rods."

then what will you do with them?"

'i't know. Haven't thought that far."

made them on the spur of the moment because
ln't resist it?"

)ose . . . Yes."

or thought.

:," I said, "the thing to do is make those two the
int and then decide what to do with them?"

. . . But is it worth it?"

ras the question he really wanted me to answer?

)o you mean, is it worth you making them, or
th making?"

uess," he said.

in my opinion, yes. It's worth you making
are worth making."

"Why?"

Oh, please, I thought, just do it! Don't question so much!

And I was beginning to feel down. I'd forgotten the aftereffects of the 'flu during our happy meal and finding out what Karl was doing. But now started to feel queasy again.

I don't know how I'd have answered his question because before I could try there was a knock on the door.

This injected a supercharge of energy into Karl, who shot off the workbench and grabbed the door handle, while shouting, "Don't come in! Go away! Don't come in."

And Mrs. Williamson's shocked voice replying, "I won't. I've brought you some coffee."

"All right!" Karl shouted. "Put it down. I'll get it. Don't come in. Go away."

And Mrs. Williamson saying, "Yes, all right. I'm going. I'm going."

Karl waited, then opened the door enough to check his mother had gone.

Now, I'm slow to anger, which is just as well, because I'm unreasonable when roused.

And Karl's behaviour roused me.

"Just a minute!" I said, or rather heard myself explode, for anger splits you in two, or at least it does me. The angry me being angry and the normal me observing the angry me being angry.

was beside Karl and pushing him away before I could
myself.

What!" Karl said.

ut I paid no heed, opened the door and called after Mrs.
amson's retreating figure, "Wait, Mrs. Williamson.
wait!"

t she went on into the house.

sed the door and confronted Karl and in a stern voice
him and rare to myself said, "That was disgraceful!"

at!"

should be ashamed of yourself!"

then in a voice that matched mine, he said, "What
are you talking about?"

was your mother, for God's sake."

't want her in here."

lon't talk to your mother like that. Never! Not for
."

e enraged bull to bull, close up.

nothing to do with you," he said.

stand by and say nothing when you behave so
ur mother."

of your business."

ver interfered in your *business* before?"

er criticised you in any way?"

er told you you were wrong?"

Karl turned away and leaned against the workbench.

I waited. Nothing.

"Have the decency to give me a reply."

"All right!" Karl said with a wave of the hand that would have pushed me away had I been in range. "All right. No."

I made myself calm down before saying, "Then give me some credit for that and listen to me now."

"I don't want her in here, that's all."

"Why not?"

"I don't want her seeing what I'm doing."

"Why not? You invited me to see it."

"That's different."

"How?"

"I thought you'd understand."

"And your mother wouldn't?"

"Yes! No! No, she wouldn't."

The anger drained from both of us. I sat down and we declined into silence.

Now I was upset with myself for losing my temper.

They say you should never apologise and never explain, because it shows a sign of weakness.

Baloney.

That's the cause of vendettas, endless cycles of revenge and the interminable abomination of war.

And I know something else. It's the older, and the stranger, who must break the circle.

I forced myself to say, "I'm sorry. I lost my temper."

Karl said nothing. Nor did I want him to. Mutual

ogies don't heal the wound, they only put a bandage
it.
aid, "Do something for me."
rl remained silent.
et me ask your mother to join us. Show her what
done and see what she says."
reply.
t yourself in her shoes, Karl. You're her only son.
ly child. She adores you. Quite literally, she'd die for
hink you know that. She's gone through a hell of
bout you these last few months. Now she sees her
son full of life again. And it's obvious whatever has
d has something to do with what you're doing in
n't you think you ought to show her? Even if she
nderstand. Isn't it the right thing to do?"
e remained silent, but took a deep, deep breath
out as if he were expelling poisoned air.
noments passed again before I said, "Shall I go
?"
led.

e was upset, Jane used to talk about "crying
ought of that when I found Mrs. Williamson
e kitchen table, no longer chirpy, no longer
roman she had been during our meal, and
out her betraying how hurt she felt. There
in her eyes, but I was sure she was crying

I sat down at the table, opposite her.

I said, "Karl wants you to join us in the shed."

She said, head down and with an effort, "I hoped we were through with this."

I said, "I think you are."

She let out a heavy sigh.

"Then why . . ."

"I think this is different."

She looked at me, a hard angry look I hadn't seen from her before.

"Different?" she said. "What's different about it?"

"He was rude. I know. But I don't think he meant to be. I don't think he meant to hurt you. Or reject you."

"That's certainly how it felt."

"Yes."

"Well, then?"

"I can only tell you how it seems to me. I'm not saying I'm right."

She didn't respond. For the first time I wondered whether Karl's reticence, whether his refusal to speak when he was upset or facing a difficulty in himself, came from his mother, and not, as I'd assumed, from his father. Maybe he wasn't so much his father's child as his mother's boy?

I said, "This didn't happen because he's depressed again. It happened because he isn't ready to show you what he's doing in the shed."

"He showed you. Why not me? Do I mean so much less to him?"

No! Just the opposite."

e gave a huffy laugh.

He showed it to me because I don't mean to him what
o."

Well, I'm glad you understand it, because I certainly
"

aited a moment to let the sparks die.

en I said, "When I was starting out as a writer, I hated
ng anyone what I was writing before I'd finished it. I
 that if they said it was no good, I'd feel so crushed I'd
p. Especially if it was my parents who didn't like it.
when I finished it I didn't want my parents to read it.
l someone else had said it was OK. Someone whose
n my parents respected."

. Williamson gave me a searching look.

he writing something then?"

."

 what is he doing?"

ink that's for him to tell you."

d he's sent you to fetch me?"

"

y couldn't he come for me himself?"

too hard for him."

 didn't have any difficulty telling me to go away."

ow I knew she was being deliberately stubborn. Of
she understood! She was an intelligent woman. She
er son. She'd been through worse than this with
was pretty sure this wasn't the first time he'd been

rude to her. I knew what it was like when you were in the pit of depression. You want the person closest to you to attend, but at the same time you want to be left alone. An emotional double bind. And you are hurting so much you can't help passing the hurt on.

Mrs. Williamson knew this. But Karl seemed to be out of the pit now, and she had been shocked by his behaviour because she feared it meant he'd reverted. What's more, there was hurt from those bad months locked up inside her, where she'd kept it while Karl was ill so as not to make things worse, and to show him that nothing he did, however bad, would turn her away from him or cause her to treat him as badly as he had treated her. She thought this was over, but his sudden rudeness had churned the pent-up bile, which she couldn't help letting out a bit on me.

As for Karl, now that he was his best self again and something was happening to him he only half understood—something bright and new he didn't yet know how to deal with—he was protecting himself in case this bright new thing was taken from him before he'd grasped it.

And me? I was an outsider, sympathetic to both mother and son. And quite often an outsider can see what's going on between two people when the two people are blind to it.

There was something else I thought I understood, but didn't mention to Mrs. Williamson.

Karl is an only son and I'm an only son. I've known others during my life. And have observed that they—we—tend to behave in one of two ways with our mothers. Some

eeply attached, tell their mother everything, and do
ng without discussing it with her. Others keep their
ce, are reserved, tell their mothers as little as possible
 what they are doing. I was of the second kind. And
w I knew Karl was too.

 unless you're intent on deliberately hurting your
r, which I never was and I believed Karl wasn't, there
ne important things in your life you have to reveal.
st as I had to tell my mother I was trying to be a
because of how hurt I knew she would be if I didn't,
ew it was necessary for Karl to explain to his mother
e was trying to do that made him closet himself
ely in the shed. I was sure he had to do this because
ft revealing what I was up to till it was too late.
ach this caused between myself and my mother was
paired. I didn't want that to happen to Karl.

w if it went wrong, neither of them would have
 more to do with me.

 you go and see?" I asked.
niled and said, "Course I will! Did you think for
d that I wouldn't?"
ed.
re friends again.
 up.
oing to, but suddenly felt quite done in.
Villiamson waited. "Are you all right? You don't
od."

"The bloody 'flu," I said. "Overdone it a bit, first day out. Enjoyed myself too much."

"Have a lie down on the sofa in the sitting room."

"Kind of you. But, if you don't mind, I think I'll just slope off home and go to bed."

"You sure? Shall I get Karl to drive you?"

"No, no. You go and see him. Very important. I'll manage. Really. Say good-bye to him for me, and tell him I'm sorry to duck out but I'll be in touch."

"Of course! And you're sure you'll be OK?"

"I will. Honestly."

As soon as I got home, I went to bed and was a goner for the next five hours. When I woke, I felt like I'd been squashed by an avalanche.

# NINETEEN

------

A SUNDAY, I MADE A BET WITH MYSELF THAT MRS.
ɔn would phone to ask how I was.

way, how do you make a bet with yourself? With
you betting? This brings me back to that endlessly
ndlessly fascinating question: When I'm talking
whom am I talking to and who is doing the
? we all in fact two people, not one? Are we all
ιother? What I know is that I have an "everyday
e who does things, says things, deals with the
ups and downs of daily life, and another, an
:he one I think of as my real self, the self who
ithing my everyday self does, comments and
and dispraises, considers what would be best
to do, and assesses the results.

one of me bet Mrs. W. would phone is the
(But won what?)

195

Typical of her thoughtfulness, she waited till late morning, in case, as she said, I wanted to sleep in.

We exchanged the usual routine conversational strokes: How was I this morning? Much better, thank you. And her? Very well, thank you. Had I recovered from yesterday? Yes, and how much I'd enjoyed our meal. And how much she had too.

Those pleasantries out of the way, I asked whether she had gone to see Karl in the shed.

Yes, she had.

What did she make of what she saw?

She'd been so surprised, she didn't know what to think.

So what had she said?

Nothing. She didn't have to. As soon as she'd looked at the things on the workbench, Karl told her they were little models.

"I said, 'Models of what?' He said they were models of sculptures he was thinking of making full sized. I asked him where he got the idea from. He said he'd seen some sculptures when he went with you the other day, and he just felt he wanted to make something like them. So he was trying out some ideas with bits of wire because it would be too expensive to experiment with metal tubes and rods."

"And what did you say?"

"I asked him why he hadn't wanted me to know what he was doing. He said he didn't want to show me till he was sure it wasn't a passing fad. So I asked why he'd

vn them to you. He said you'd understand what he
trying to do, and it wouldn't matter so much if he
up after that. I asked him why he'd decided to show
ow. Did that mean he'd go on? He said you'd told
t was wrong to show you and not to show me. He
e hadn't meant to hurt me, but if I'd not liked
ie was doing it would upset him and put him off.
I understood now why he hadn't told me. I was
was doing something that made him happy and
! he'd go on with it, and I'd help him any way
We gave each other a hug and that was that. I
:k into the house and Karl went on working in
"

"So you didn't talk about the models?"
Mrs. W. said. "Which was just as well, because I
ave known what to say. They just looked like bits
e to me."
That's all they are, in a way."
laughed and said, "I'm sure he thinks they're
hat, but what? Do you know?"
iure yet."
t tell you?"
:ss they represent ideas. Feelings. Thoughts."
i abstract art?"
it to call it that."
o good with abstract art. I like art that looks
iow."
it people do."

197

"And you?"

"I like some and not all. I think some of it is a load of old tosh. Pretentious nonsense. Some of it is wonderful. But that's true of everything, isn't it?"

Pause.

Mrs. W. said, "D'you think he wants to be a sculptor? I mean professionally?"

"I've no idea."

"He hasn't said?"

"And I haven't asked."

"But if he does, won't he have to go to art school, to learn how to do it properly?"

"Not necessarily. He could find a job as an assistant to a sculptor and learn that way."

"You mean, like an apprenticeship? Like he learned his plumbing?"

"Why not? That's the way it used to be done for centuries, till we all got hung up on going to college and getting bits of paper to prove we're supposed to be able to do something we learn best by doing it."

"But isn't it hard to make a living as a sculptor?"

"Harder than making a living as a plumber, that's for sure."

"Oh dear!"

Pause.

"Will you encourage him, if he decides to do it as a job?" Mrs. W. said, her voice giving away her worry.

"You'd rather I didn't?"

Wouldn't he be better off as a plumber and doing his
ɔting as a hobby?"

Well, let's see how things develop."

ut you'll not push him into it?"

Io, I'll not push him into anything."

ıse.

ıere's something else," Mrs. W. said.

hat's that?"

had another visitor yesterday, not long after you'd

ɔ"

ella."

*lla!* What did she want?"

:e Karl of course."

ʼ?"

le her wait while I asked him. He told me to send
shed."

ɔthing! Karl came in about an hour later. I asked
Fiorella was. He said she left by the back gate. I
she wanted. He said, just to see him. I asked if
her his models. He said he had."

t was it?"

s it. You know my Karl well enough by now.
want to tell you something, wild horses won't
ʼhim."

ʼs a turnup for the book!"

This bolt of news rather knocked me off balance. What was Fiorella up to? And what was Karl up to, allowing her to see his models? And what else went on between them? And why had she chosen that day to drop in on him uninvited? Or was she uninvited? Had something gone on between them which Karl preferred I didn't know about? I felt pretty sure he'd have mentioned it, had he and Fiorella got together again. Or would he?

To be truthful, I felt miffed that he might be keeping something like this from me. But I knew, at the same time, there was no reason why he should confide in me—about this or anything else. And I had to confess to myself that feeling miffed was a sign that I was assuming too much, expecting too much, of our friendship, and that I was more concerned about him, and wanted to be closer to him, than I should allow myself to want.

The only thing I could think to say was, "Where is he now?"

But the way I said it gave away my too-keen interest.

"Gone fishing," Mrs. W. said.

I thought it best not to go any further. And she must have thought so too, because she added,

"Is there anything you need? Anything I can bring for you?"

I said, no, thanks, I was OK.

Pause.

'You can call me anytime," she said.

knew she meant to reassure me.

Ve went though the usual chatter before ringing off.

thought that would be it for the rest of the day and

d down to read the Sunday papers. But no.

# TWENTY

-------

THAT AFTERNOON, I CHECKED MY EMAILS. THIS FROM FIORELLA:

As you know *everything* about Karl, you are bound
to know what he is doing with bits of wire. I went to
see him yesterday. I know I said I wouldn't. I know
he doesn't like surprises. (I think he is probably
a control freak.) But I couldn't help myself, I was
desperate to see him, I wish I wasn't but I was, I
mean I still am. I thought he wouldn't see me but
he did. He was in the garden shed. I wouldn't say
he was exactly ecstatic. Very arm's-length and
hands-off, when what I wanted was close-up and
intimate and hands-on. As a matter of fact, most
of the time I was there I felt I was being watched,
being *observed*, like I was some kind of laboratory
specimen. Also like I was being *tested* and *assessed*

202

nd *examined*. I tried to be cool and offhand and
ll that but when I'm unsure of myself I start to
abble, yammer yammer yammer. I do wish I
dn't do this. It is so *gauche*. I know I'm doing it
the time and keep telling myself to *shut up*, but
't stop myself, can't help it, it really is a pain.
 went on blathering at him, it doesn't matter
t I said, about nothing really. And he just stood
e listening and watching and *saying nothing*.
 after *an age* he asked me why I'd come—I
ecause I wanted to see him, no other reason—
e asked how I was getting on—school, chess,
lah. I asked about him but he did that trick
wering my questions with questions about
id instead of pushing him to talk about
 I stupidly rabbitted on again about myself.
 do this, with him anyway, because what I
int to do is get hold of him and etc. etc.
ust something about him that makes
 to do that, there's something small boy
rable about him and at the same time
 terribly grown-up and strong and I have
ind that combination plus his looks, his
 irresistible. I guess blathering on is a
pensation or something for not being
ouch him and hold him. I suppose I'm
ich him and hold him and kiss him

Now I'm rabbitting on to you and not getting to the point. Why am I doing that? It's important to know why you do what you do, especially the things you do without meaning to, don't you agree? I know you agree because all your books are like that, which is one reason why I like them. So why am I rabbitting on to you now? (Pause for thought.) Oh dear, I don't like what I'm thinking. (Pause for more thought.) Well, alright, what it is, I think, is—I don't know how to put it without sounding stupid or bitchy—but I half resent you knowing Karl better than I do and seeing him all the time and I don't, and half resent Karl knowing you and seeing you, because after all he only got to know you because of me talking to him about your books (which he hasn't read, by the way, I know because I asked him yesterday, but then, you know he doesn't read novels or anything he doesn't have to, but only what he really wants to, and why he doesn't). Does this mean I'm jealous? I hope it doesn't. I hate the thought that I might be a jealous person. It's such an ugly weakness. And am I being like some silly girl who comes wittering on because she thinks she's been left out of the game and wants to worm her way in and be best friends with the other two and goes smarming up to them trying to ingratiate herself? God, I hope not!

The only way to stop wittering like this is to stop

wittering. So:

LONG PAUSE FOR RECOVERY OF CALM.

*Much later.*

Here is my point in best exam-essay style:

 had not been in Karl's shed, which he called

workshop, before, so everything in it was new

 e. To stop myself blathering on I asked about

 use of some of the tools and machines. Karl

 ed briefly. There were some bits of wire on

 orkbench, which I didn't take any notice of,

 se I thought they were bits of rubbish. All the

 Karl was standing at the end of the bench,

 back against it.

 ng looked round the shed (sorry, workshop),

 ing he would allow me to get close now that

 gone round the houses with reconnecting

 I ended my tour beside him, intending to

 nst the bench in the same posture as him.

 id this he said with alarm, Hey! Careful!

 is hand on my back to stop me leaning

 e bench.

 nt thought was that he did this because

 ant me so close to him. But in the next

 alised he was keeping me from maybe

 e bits of wire.

 t say anything, just kept looking at me

 server's eye. I felt he was waiting for

me to say something special, something important, but I couldn't think what it was. Again, I felt I was being tested.

Of course I understood from what he'd done that these bits of wire weren't just bits of rubbish.

Thinking it would please him if I showed some interest, I reached out to pick one up, but he caught me by the wrist and said, Don't touch! (Come to think of it, this could be taken as the motto for the day.)

I said I was sorry and asked if they were something special. He said they were. I asked why. He said they were little models. I asked what of. He said, What do you think? I said I had no idea. And instantly felt a dreadful failure, which made me want to run away, but I was determined not to let him get the better of me. Which is another thing about him. He is very powerful.

Anyway and anyhow I said I didn't know and Karl said, Guess.

Well, I thought, I'm not going to play this game, I've had enough of it.

I said, You're being horrible to me.

He said, No, I'm not.

I said, Yes, you are. I came to see you, to find out how you are, because I know you haven't been too great lately, and you're treating me like I'm something the cat dragged in, like a *child*, and like

ou're some kind of teacher condescending to a
upid pupil. You are *patronising me* and I don't
e it!

Have a guess, he said, as if I hadn't uttered a
ord.

That really did me in!

I said, sharp as I could, I have no idea what you
an or what these nasty-looking bits of wire are
. And to be honest, Karl, I don't care.

He smiled then. The observer look vanished. He
tched his head. And then said, all politeness
public good manners, Sorry if I upset you.
d of you to call. I'm OK. Doing well, thanks.

Vhich meant, clear as day, the visit was over.
didn't exactly go to the door and open it, but
night as well have done.

aid, See you around, and left by the back gate
oid Mrs. Williamson and her questions.

, Mr. Writer. What's going on? What is so
al about those bits of wire?

ase tell me.

*ave* to know.

ur reader, Fiorella

days, everyone expects instant replies—to emails,
gs, tweets, and who knows what else has been
the techno list before you read this sentence?

v Fiorella would be checking her inbox every

few minutes. But decided not to submit to the universal imperative for the instantaneous. She could wait, while I decided what to say to her. If anything.

And it's just as well I did.

# Twenty-one

-------

'CLOCK. SIXTEEN HUNDRED HOURS. THE FRONT DOORBELL.
lling. No callers without appointment. No one had
intment.
d from my workroom window. The top of Karl's
iew.
I opened the door, he was holding out to his
ciform, one in each hand, a couple of trout, his
with a broad grin.
supper," he said. "I'll cook it, if you like."
t the fish in the kitchen sink, asked to use the
, returned, washed and brushed up and burnished
in river air, his outdoor gear removed, back in
on uniform of black crewneck sweater and jeans.
work cleaning and gutting the fish, preparing
d salad.
he kitchen table and watched.

"How are you feeling?" he asked.

"Fine. And to what do I owe the honour of this visit?"

"I brought you the fish," he said, scrubbing away, but he wasn't a good liar. There was a giveaway wobble in his voice.

"I can tell there's something. So stop fussing with the fish and come clean."

A tense moment. I could feel him holding himself down. Then he swilled his hands under the tap and dried them on a towel. He turned to me, but didn't look at me. "I want to know," came out in a burst, "what you think."

Typical Karl! Fill in the gaps. He was an expert at indeterminacy.

"About your models and making sculptures?"

He nodded, still no eye contact.

I said, "I've thought a lot about that since yesterday."

"And?"

"I'm glad you've come. There's something I want to show you. And then I have a couple of questions."

I led him out into the front garden, where I sat on the sitting room windowsill and indicated to him to sit beside me. There was just enough daylight left.

"Look at the garden," I said. "What do you see?"

"What d'you mean?"

"What I say. What do you see?"

He looked. Shook his head.

"Well. The garden. The lawn. A border of lavender along the path. The wall with the road on the other side . . . I dunno! . . . What am I supposed to see?"

walked to the centre of the lawn. And stooped over,
arm bent over my neck, the other arm stuck straight up
angle, and peered at him from under that arm.

wasn't an easy pose to hold. But I managed to stay
long enough for the brow-wrinkled puzzlement on
face to be wiped clean by the dawn of perception.

d then, both of us realising the ridiculousness of my
rted pose, we spluttered into laughter.

ncurled myself and returned to the windowsill.

id, "I'll pay for the materials."

unhurried pause.

ore Karl said, "I don't know what to say."

d, "I'd say, yes, thank you, if I were you."

t what if you don't like it?"

'll make a model first?"

need to."

en we can go step by step."

a good place."

's the right size. And shape as well, of course."

ld fit the garden. And be good against the view of
y."

I could look down at it from my workroom, which
ve another angle."

another from the bottom of the garden and the
king towards the house."

hat do you say?"

ather than heard his chuckle.

ught some more.

Then, parodying me, "Yes, thank you."

"Done!" I said. "Let's go back inside. I shall get piles, if I sit on this cold ledge much longer."

As we went in, I suggested he get on with the cooking while we talked.

I sat at the table, and said, "There's a few things I'd like to ask you."

"Go ahead."

"Are you thinking of becoming a professional sculptor?"

"And nothing else?"

"Yes."

"No."

"So it's a hobby?"

"No."

"Explain."

"I do want to make sculptures. I've been doing a lot of looking on the internet. I'm getting an idea of what's possible. And I do want to show them. Like the ones we saw at the hotel. In natural places, not art galleries. And I'll sell them if anybody wants them, which I doubt."

"You haven't made any yet, so you can't know."

"Yeah, but."

"That sounds like being a professional to me."

"But I want to keep on being a plumber."

"OK. I can see you need to make a living. But if you make it as a sculptor?"

"I don't know if I can explain this very well. I've only

ght of it these last few days. And I haven't talked to
ody about it."

this why you came to see me today?"

es."

n privileged."

ah, yeah!"

nean it. So try me."

ell . . . Sculpture is, like, an art, isn't it?"

an art, yes."

on't know anything about art. I've never thought
bout it. But what I think is art is kind of personal, if
ow what I mean? Artists do it to please themselves,
ey?"

can put it like that. I'd say the best artists, and the
ists, do it because they have to."

mean, they can't help it?"

don't feel they have any choice about it."

't quite get what you mean."

see . . . You had a choice about becoming a
You could have been an electrician or a carpenter
g like that. Yes?"

I'm trying to say is some people do things because
ey have to. Some people paint pictures or make
because they want to. They choose to do it. But
le do it because they feel that's what they *must*

an, like it's their fate?"

213

"I'm not keen on thinking of it as fate, but it'll do for now."

"But still . . . What are they doing . . . with it?"

"They aren't doing anything *with it*. They're just making something. Making an object."

"Like you tried to explain to me the other day?"

"That's it."

"But why?"

"Why did you make those models? Why do you want to make them into sculptures?"

He finished what he was doing and sat down.

"I don't know!"

There was desperation in his voice.

"Do you need to know?"

"Yes!"

"Tell me if I'm wrong, but I'm guessing you feel you can't help doing it."

"Sort of. Yes."

"Isn't it enough to know you can't help it?"

"No!"

"Maybe you can't know why you have to do it until you've done it. And done it more than once or twice but many times. Maybe it's by doing it you find out why you're doing it."

"But you must have some idea why real artists do it."

"I think there are probably a number of reasons."

"All right. Give me one."

I didn't want to. I didn't want him to think the reason I gave was the best or the only worthy reason.

Come on," he said, almost violently. "Tell me!"

ll right, all right! . . . I think the main reason is that it's
nly way they know how to make sense of themselves
he only way they can make sense of life. It's the only
they know how to say something about themselves
out life they feel they *need* to say."

looked at me with the kind of hard stare that's
ing. Fiorella was right. He had a power that could
ou. It was like there was a generator inside that had
nning at low power all the time I'd known him and
w revved up to full capacity.

hat how it is for you?" he said.

n't want to answer.

?"

ded.

id, sharp as acid, "Strikes me you're saying you do
yourself alive."

put a stop on me. It had taken me years as a writer
understood this about myself, yet Karl was saying
was simple and obvious.

up and went on with the cooking.

few minutes he said, "I don't want to do something
for myself all the time. I want to do something
ll. Something that's ordinary and practical and
other people. I want to make sculptures, but I
on plumbing too."

n't think sculpture is practical and useful?"

he same way plumbing is. People really need

215

plumbers, don't they? It's not much good having sculptures if your house is flooding or you've got no water, is it?"

I'd had enough philosophising about art for one night so I didn't take up the challenge. Let him think it out for himself.

He turned to me with his fish slice in his hand like a weapon.

"Well, is it?"

"I take your point."

"I want to do both. If you're talking about what I *need* to do, I need to do both."

"Even if you were a successful sculptor you'd still want to be a plumber?"

"Yes, that's what I'm saying, OK?"

"I'm not trying to dissuade you. In fact, I think it's admirable."

He turned back to his cooking. "You do?"

"I do. I think I understand what you mean. I think what you're saying is that going on with plumbing isn't about making a living, though it will do that. It's about you not losing touch with everyday life and ordinary people."

"And because I think I'll be a better sculptor the better I am as a plumber."

"And vice versa?"

"That as well."

Enough! We'd said enough. Say more and we'd kill it.

To make a break I did something I hadn't done since I

a boy. I drink wine and don't like beer. Karl preferred
. I have an old jug that belonged to my grandfather,
ather's father. Before dinner he used to fill the jug with
from his own little barrel (a firkin he kept in the dining
). When my father, who told me about this, was big
ζh to hold the jug when it was full, my grandfather
m do it. After he told me this story, my dad let me
once, by taking the jug to the local pub, filling it and
ng it back for my father. Just so I'd done it too.
ν I took the jug, which I've always treasured and
ised in case it was broken, went to the pub up the
nd brought it back full of beer for Karl.
s halfway home when I remembered that I'd said
ing to Karl's mother during his crisis about how
helped me to survive. Maybe Mrs. W. had told him
ybe he wasn't so clever after all. Maybe he was only
ζ what his mother had told him I'd said.
hen I thought, So what? Which of us ever has
ıal thought, however clever we are? I haven't.
ıg I say that's worth saying I've come across
re else—have heard it or read it. Why should I
the less of Karl for doing the same? At least he'd
ed and said it on an appropriate occasion. That's
ugh. Or maybe, maybe after all, he hadn't been
ıis mother and really had thought it for himself.

Karl some of the beer, gratified by his pleasure
done. And while he finished cooking, I excused

myself—extending the break and the silence—went to my workroom and fiddled with some papers, shelved a few stray books, returning to the kitchen when Karl shouted up the stairs that our meal was ready.

By unspoken mutual agreement we said no more then about art or his plans.

I was tempted to ask him about Fiorella. I was dying to know why he had treated her the way she described and to hear his side of the story. I hoped he might bring it up. But he didn't and I couldn't find a way of mentioning her without him wondering why and it being obvious she had been in touch.

So the evening ended with questions secluded in the air.

# TWENTY-TWO
- - - - - - -

ᴳHT, BEFORE SHUTTING DOWN THE COMPUTER ON THE
ᵇed, I checked my emails.
her from Fiorella:

ᵒu receive my email this afternoon? In case
idn't, here it is again.

ᵉ spur of the moment and without giving it a
ought, I clicked Reply and wrote:

ᵣtefact.

ᵃs as keen a reader of my books as she said she
ᵒuldn't have much trouble working out what I

# TWENTY-THREE

- - - - - - -

FOR THE NEXT THREE WEEKS I HEARD NOTHING FROM KARL.

Mrs. W. phoned every two or three days to ask after me, and keep me up to date. Karl was plumbing full-time now, eating "like there was no tomorrow," sleeping "like a baby." A complete change from the bad times. He spent his evenings in his workshop. He said nothing about what he was doing. On Sundays he went fishing. But he wasn't seeing friends or anyone and she was worried in case he became reclusive and too self-absorbed. As someone who prefers to be on my own I had nothing to offer by way of advice or sympathy.

Fiorella hadn't shown up again. Karl hadn't mentioned her. But that didn't mean they hadn't been in touch by what Mrs. W. called "virtual chat."

Late in the morning of the fourth Sunday after our fish

er, Karl phoned. Could he come over and show me
thing?

e arrived on his bike at two. He had his backpack.
a he came inside, he took out a cardboard box, which
down on the kitchen table and out of which he took
knew at once was the model of the sculpture for my
garden.

ached to the base was a little paper plaque on which
itten "Fishing for Words."

uld see what he intended. Wires that would be
ods rose up from various irregular points round the
base. The wires were shaped like lines cast from
rods, curving up into the air at irregular heights,
ught in mid-flight and some turning down into
By their overlapping they formed a kind of net.
e base was a bowl, which, as I looked, Karl filled
er. Then I saw how the ends of some of the lines
ito the water.

ly to give you an idea," Karl said. "I'll make the
ifferent metals, like black rods and stainless steel
r so they catch the light differently. That'll give
lour. And I'm going to cut letters out of a sheet
nd I'll burnish them to give them different tones
d scatter them in the bottom of the pool. And
e pool will be a birdbath. I thought of including
coming up from the middle that would burst
p of the lines so that there was a spray of
ter as well, and that would make everything

shine wet in the sunlight. I could plumb in the water supply."

I said, "It's brilliant!" And I meant it.

The model was only a hint. But I could imagine the finished thing and was touched and excited by the way he'd combined his love of fishing with my love of words, and the idea of writing being like fishing, and how he'd given the sculpture a practical use that included natural life. In a way, the thing was like a birdcage without being a cage. He'd planned the way the lines crossed and crisscrossed to leave plenty of spaces for smaller birds to get in and out without feeling trapped.

I said, "A lot will depend how big the real one is, and the proportions, don't you think?"

"I wondered if we could work out how big it should be?"

We talked this over and ended up in the front garden with a couple of kitchen chairs, arranging them on top of each other and on their sides and upside down and all such combinations, measuring the results with a tape measure, trying to work out the best dimensions. Finally, we got some sticks of bamboo I used for runner beans and did what we could to mock up a grid the height and footprint we thought would be about right for the sculpture.

We were at it for over an hour. But at last felt we had cracked it. We'd agreed the precise spot on the lawn, the height and diameter, the area and depth of the birdbath and how to construct it. And came back inside after clearing

feeling cold from the chill of the winter evening but
ling with excitement.

all our times together so far, this was the first time I felt
ere enjoying ourselves, without strain or any sense of
nce of age or of deference, concession or inequality.
, I thought afterwards, the first time we had met as
es, untrammelled, unguarded and in tune.

s glad Karl set off for home as soon as we finished
g. To have gone on would have risked blemish.

# TWENTY-FOUR

-------

THE IDEA FOR THE PARTY WAS MRS. WILLIAMSON'S. SHE SAID it was to celebrate the installation of Karl's first sculpture. I'm sure she meant it, but I'm also sure she used it as an excuse to bring together with Karl some of the friends he'd neglected since the onset of his crisis six months ago.

His pals from the rugby club came, and his boss from work, Mr. Cooksley, and, I was surprised to find, Fiorella, who brought her friend Becky, no doubt for moral support, though it crossed my mind that the typical combination of pretty (Fiorella) and plain (Becky) was meant to work to Fiorella's advantage.

When Mrs. W. first mooted it, I wasn't keen. My energy sank to zero at the prospect of the preparations as well as the party itself. But in order to please her, I agreed, assuming that Karl in his present mood wouldn't. When she told me he had, I swore to myself and asked how she'd

e it. To which I received an enigmatic "mothers have
: ways."

didn't find out till the day of the party what her
er's way was. A midday event so that there'd be
;h daylight for inspection of the installation before
inter evening set in. Mrs. W. was titivating the food
:ink in the kitchen. I was hovering with Karl in the
room. Karl was upset because he hadn't had time
he sculpture permanently. The rods were still loose,
:ing each other just enough to keep them in place.
iope to heaven there isn't a strong puff of wind or
le shebang will collapse," Karl said.) He planned to
ck the next day to fix it permanently.
d to the stress and strain, we were both suffering
:ward moments before a party when everything is
you're waiting for the guests to arrive, wondering
turn up and how you'll get through it, when Karl
y did you let her do this?"
said. "It's not my fault! Why did you?"
;ht you'd say no."
hought you would."
You said yes because you thought I'd say no?"
1 said yes because you thought I'd say no?"
computation of one and one.
id she ask you?" Karl said.
l.
before she asked me."

225

"And she didn't tell you I'd said yes?"

"No, she didn't."

"And if she had?"

"I'd have said no way!"

"Well, I'll be jiggered!"

Karl grinned at me. "You still haven't cottoned on to my mother, have you?"

"What d'you mean?"

"You think she's as nice as pie, straight as a die, and wouldn't say boo to a goose."

"Do I?"

"But it's a front. My dad used to say she was more canny than a con man and trickier than a conjuror. As innocent as a dove, he said, and as cunning as a serpent."

"Are you saying she's unscrupulous?"

"Wouldn't go as far as that. She's clever at getting what she wants. But she does have her limits."

"Does she?"

"She knows how to twist you round her little finger, that's for sure. Plays the fading flower and you fall for it."

"Me naïve? I'm shocked!"

"You fall for it because you want to. I can tell by the way you look at her."

"So this is a day for telling truths."

"She's just as bad about you. I'd go for it, if I was you."

"Don't be so ridiculous."

"I wouldn't mind, if that's what's holding you back."

"Nothing is holding me back. But even if you're right,

226

:h you're not, think of your mother's age and mine. She
1 be my daughter."
What's that got to do with it?"
More than you can yet know, young man."
es, Granddad."
ckily at that moment the first guests arrived. A
mage of Karl's rugger pals.

we had a party.
adapt a well-known quotation: All happy parties are
ne, each unhappy party is unhappy in its own way.
he time, this seemed to me to be a happy party.
n not making things up and it is not a novel but
ount of events in real life, all I can say is that
the party everyone seemed to me to behave
far as behaving well at parties goes. Karl's sculp-
s admired, though not without some teasing by
er pals, and the guests departed without over-
heir welcome and before the food and drink ran

aid, there was one incident that might have marred
edings. We were all out in the garden viewing the
Mrs. W. insisted, much to Karl's discomfit, that
a glass to Karl's work." We did as instructed. At
ent a gang of young men were sloping by on the
of beer in their hands, and well oiled with booze.
ed them at once: the same four who sat next to
oub and riled Karl the night of the fracas. They

saw us, stopped, jeered, blew raspberries, and indicated by various gestures what we should do with ourselves.

Karl bridled at this. As did his rugger pals. War would undoubtedly have been declared were it not for the intervention of Karl's boss, Mr. Cooksley, who announced in the stentorian tones of a sergeant major on the parade ground, which outclassed the baying of the yobs by a good margin of decibels, "Steady, the Buffs!"*

I doubt very much that Karl or his pals had heard this ancient command before. But the manner of its delivery carried such authority and its meaning was so plain that it had the effect of restraining Karl and his pals and, more astonishingly, silencing the yobs, who wandered on their inebriated way with a few yeowls and whoops to save face.

* Karl and his pals might not have heard this before, but I had. It was common in my childhood as a warning not to take any impulsive action you might regret or would be inappropriate at the time. I didn't know then, though I do now, that it originated in 1858 on the island of Malta, where the 2nd Battalion, the Royal East Kent Regiment, was stationed. The regiment was one of oldest in the British Army, dating back to 1572. They were called "the Buffs" because at one time their uniforms were made of light brown leather. In 1858 they were quartered with the Royal North British Fusiliers, with whom there was some rivalry. One day on the parade ground, this rivalry would have led to competitive unseemliness, but it was forestalled by the very strict Royal Kent adjutant, a Scot named Cotter, who brooked no disobedience. He called out, "Steady, the Buffs!" and the brewing trouble was dispelled. From that day the Royal Kents used this as their battle cry, until in 1961 the regiment was amalgamated with others and is today part of the Princess of Wales Royal Regiment. I offer this item of useless information for your edification and amusement.

ter which, with huffs and smiles and raised eyebrows
the older of us, and some rumbling irritation among
ounger, the party continued with pretended disregard
interruption.

er, when I tackled him about it, I gathered from Mr.
sley that he'd spent eleven years in the army, where
ched the rank of warrant officer, which explained his
and timely intervention.

were looking at Karl's sculpture.

hat d'you think?" I asked him.

ot my cup of tea, to be honest," he said.

u don't like it?"

well made. But so it should be!" He smiled. "I
him."

you're not too keen?"

on't see what he's trying to do. I like pictures,
es, that sort of thing, to look like they are meant

means it to be what he feels. About fishing. What
eels like. What it means to him."

l, it's beyond me. But I'll tell you this. I'm pleased
to do it. His dad would have been pleased as well."

knew his dad."

as my best friend. Grew up together. Same schools.
rainier than me. Went off and did engineering at
uilt up his business. But never forgot where he
n. Never any airs and graces. And never forgot his
ls."

"You must miss him."

"You could say."

"And Karl. You must have known him since he was born."

"I was with his dad in the maternity ward the night he arrived."

"So, since his father died, you must have been like a second father to him."

Mr. Cooksley gave a huffing smile. "No, no! Nobody could replace him. I've never seen a father and son so close. Did everything together from day one. Too close. I used to think it wasn't good for a lad to be that attached. And I was right. The loss of his dad devastated him."

"But you've been a big help."

"Done what I could. For him and his mother. She and my wife are as good friends as his dad and I were. Boyhood sweethearts we both married. Not cool by today's standards."

"Admirable, in my view," I said, thinking of Jane and me.

Mr. Cooksley gave me a square look. "You've helped a lot. I'll say that. Sometimes takes a stranger to sort you out when you're in shtook."

"If that's right, I'm glad."

"Seems to me, the trouble is his father died while Karl was still a kid. Before he was old enough to rebel."

"Before he was a teenager?"

"Exactly. Before his balls dropped. If he had, rebelled a

mean, kicked over the traces, like most boys do when
re that age, he might have got aback of his father and
me his own man."

"Deidentified."

"that what it's called?"

y the developmental psychologists."

eally? Well, whatever it's called, he never did it."

om what you say and from what Karl has told me,
ed his father as much as one person can love another.
ot sure that's such a bad thing."

owever much you love somebody, you should always
part of yourself to yourself. Never give it all. You can
e yourself otherwise. And when his father died, Karl
d pretty much died with him. That's what's caused
uble. He's struggling to find himself. Like who he is.
ie is."

d nothing. We were on touchy ground.

at's my opinion, anyway," Mr. Cooksley said.

d, "He's told you he wants to do more sculpting?"

talked about it."

he wants to go on being a plumber. To keep his feet
round, so to speak."

Cooksley smiled.

proud of him for that," he said.

be the sculpting will help him find himself."

think so? I can't see it myself. But there's always

When everyone had gone, Mrs. Williamson, Karl and I cleared away the debris and washed up. Then Mrs. W. went off home, leaving Karl and me to return ourselves to normal. But I sensed that in some as-yet-indefinable way the party had caused a change in our friendship.

It was dark by then, and frosty. Icy, in fact, which, sitting in the warmth of my kitchen over final mugs of coffee, neither of us realised.

"That went well," I said.

"Some of it was all right," Karl said.

"Only some? Everybody liked your sculpture."

Karl huffed. "So they said."

"You didn't believe them?"

"Not all of them. Most of them thought it was just about fishing and the fish were the letters to make words."

"You mean they only took it literally?"

"They didn't get it."

"How do you know?"

"Their eyes. They said nice things. But you could tell from their eyes they didn't mean it."

"Give them a chance! People don't always catch on straightaway."

"Maybe."

He drank his coffee.

I said, "You find it hard to take compliments."

He gave me an unyielding look.

o I?" he said dismissively.

t I wasn't going to be put off.

ou shy away when you're praised," I said. "You didn't
them when they said they liked it. Would you have
d them if they'd said they didn't like it?"

obably."

hy?"

on't trust people when they're being too nice."

head went down. I knew better than to press the

ce.

n, giving me his wary sidelong look, Karl said,
did you think of Fiorella?"

I thought, now we're getting to it.

l, "Not quite what I expected."

w?"

sure of herself. Perhaps she was nervous."

y?"

ting me, perhaps."

would that bother her?"

lers often are when they meet a favourite author.
excited. And often the author doesn't live up to
ectations. At least, I don't think I do. So they end
pointed. And that makes them more nervous,
hey don't know what to say."

't think that was it."

then?"

ght have been."

"You were there as well. She was probably a bit nervous about that."

"Why?"

"Unsure how you'd treat her. Unsure what to say about your sculpture. Three reasons to be nervous. You, me, and your sculpture."

"Maybe."

"So?"

"She was a ladge."

"A ladge?"

"Yes."

"You've lost me."

"A *ladge*. You know."

"No, I don't know."

"A ladge. An embarrassment."

"That's a new one."

"No, it isn't! You should get out more."

"I told you this was a day for telling truths. So she embarrassed you?"

"Yes. You didn't notice?"

"Not particularly."

"The way she trumped around the lads? And the hyper guff about the sculpture?"

"I didn't hear. I saw you talking, but I was talking to your boss at the time."

What I didn't say, because it was so obvious there was no need, is that nothing kills love—and friendship come to that—more quickly than embarrassment.

ing not to sound too obvious about why, I asked,
t about her friend?" I'd spotted them talking for a lot
r than he and Fiorella spent together.

cky? She's OK. I like her. She said some interesting
about sculpture."

ich as?"

e asked what got me started. I told her. And she
about Tucker. William Tucker."

ally? What a coincidence!"

e's doing art history. First year at uni. King's College
n. She's a year older than Fiorella. Keen on sculpture.
derstood what I'm trying to do straightaway. Which
a certainly didn't. I didn't have to tell her. She told
e's seen a piece by Tucker at the Tate. Very minimal.
ork independent of the subject. Getting the richest
rom the simplest means. That's what I'm after. We're
o see it together."

n his vocabulary had changed: Tucker . . . A piece by
ii . . . Minimal . . . The work independent of, etc.
hest effect from, etc. . . . The Tate.

n one afternoon's conversation.

changeful power of instant recognition!

iled to myself.

o, Becky. Good-bye, Fiorella.

sped on. "She's read a book Tucker wrote about
re. Told me some of the stuff in it. Made a lot of
he's lending it to me."

at did she say about yours?"

"She made a good suggestion for how to make it better. As soon as she said it, I could have kicked myself. Should have seen it myself."

"Well, that's OK. You still can."

"Yes. A good thing I didn't have time to fix it."

"So you'll be seeing Becky again."

"She's coming to help me take the piece back home tomorrow. She'll borrow her dad's car, so I won't need to bother you."

Well, I thought, that's a step in the right direction.

But, all the same, isn't jealousy an ugly emotion!

"I'd better push off," Karl said. "Thanks for today."

"I enjoyed it. See you tomorrow."

"Becky's picking me up from work. So we'll be here about six."

It was then we heard the racket in the garden.

# Twenty-five

- - - - - - -

HEM AT ONCE, EVEN THOUGH THE ONLY LIGHT WAS THE FADED
blear from the streetlamp some way down on the
ide of the road. The four who had jeered. The
m the incident in the pub. The four brain-dead
ice thugs.

this time not even the parade-ground authority of
ant officer Cooksley would have stifled their mob-
intent.

e time Karl and I were outside and had taken in
s going on, they were ripping apart the rods from
pture and flinging them around the garden.

let out a cry of rage and launched himself in rugger-
he nearest vandal.

actively aware that this was not a wise move, I
at him to stop and set off after him, meaning to
n back. But had taken no more than a couple of

strides when one of the rods came flying at me, struck me on the chest so hard that I stumbled, my foot slipped on the icy path, and down I went, cracking my head on the stone wall dividing my garden from my neighbour's.

I came to in a hospital bed an hour or so later. For once, I can't be exact about the time.

What happened next I know only from what I was told by Mrs. Williamson and Karl himself over the next two days, and from the testimony of my next-door neighbour, Gillian, a middle-aged divorced librarian, Tom the publican from the pub up the road, and the police, during the trial of the four offenders in the magistrate's court a couple of months later.

Karl's rugger tackle brought down one of the four, who struggled to get free while yelling to his pals to "get 'im off of me." Karl was sure it was the one he'd had the barney with in the pub. (I learned the names of the four of them from the police after they were arrested. But can't use their names for legal reasons.)

The others came to his aid and hauled Karl to his feet.

But Karl, with his robust and fit 180 pounds in full flood of anger, was not a force to mess with. And though his assailants were the soul of bravery when mob-handed and timidly opposed, their emboozed physique was no match for an enraged Karl. As he twisted out of their grip their flabby condition was no protection against an elbow

ed into the brewer's gut of one, a plumber's fist jabbed
he snozzle of another and a back-footed kick into the
of the third.

e gutted one bent double, gripping his belly while he
lered the evening's intake onto his feet. The snozzled
taggered back, holding his face in his hands while
g out a sound resembling an alpine yodel. And the
ed one fell jackknifed to the ground, knees up and
gripping himself between his legs, while alternately
ing and sobbing.

is should have been the end of it. But in the time
ut with the threesome was in progress, the one Karl
lled got to his feet, grabbed a rod, and as Karl turned
his demolition job, he thrashed the rod across Karl's
g just below the knee, sending Karl sprawling to the
d, gasping with pain. He knew at once that his leg
roken and didn't try and stand.

anyone's guess whether the gang would have taken
iance to exact vengeance and cause more injury had
been for Tom the publican, alarmed by the noise,
ig to see what was going on. What he didn't know
iat Gillian had heard the noise when it started, had
it of bed and looked out of her bedroom window.
g the yobs attacking the sculpture she had called the
. And then, when she saw me collapse, had called an
lance as well.

m recognised the foursome only too well from

other episodes in his pub besides the one involving Karl. He would have tried to detain them but when he saw me comatose on the path and Karl shouting that his leg was broken, he decided it was more important to attend to us.

Gillian opened her window and shouted to Tom that she had called the police and an ambulance.

This news galvanised the foursome, distracting them enough from nursing their various bruises to hightail it out of the garden and away up the road.

The rest is straightforward. The police arrived and learned from Karl, Tom and Gillian what had happened and who the perpetrators were. The ambulance arrived moments after the police and carted Karl and me to hospital. Karl phoned his mother while we were on the way. Mrs. W. took a taxi to the hospital. She was the first person I saw when I came to.

Gillian made sure everything was secure in my house and locked up. We have keys to each other's house in case of emergency when one of us is away.

The foursome were rounded up by the police next day, appeared before the magistrates on charges of grievous bodily harm, trespass and destruction of property. They were bound over to keep the peace until their trial came to court two months later. They were found guilty, but because they had no previous convictions, and their snazzy lawyer, paid for by the local councillor father of one of

, argued they had been provoked by Karl attacking
and were only acting in self-defence, they received a
g-off by the magistrate, and were sentenced to twelve
hs' probation and one hundred hours' community
e.

# TWENTY-SIX

-------

THERE ISN'T MUCH MORE TO TELL.

As I mentioned, when I came to in the hospital, Mrs. Williamson was at my bedside. I was dazy and remember only that she made sure I was conscious and aware of where I was and what had happened to me but nothing more, before she went off to be with Karl, about whose condition she said nothing and I was still too confused to ask.

Later, a nurse told me I was suffering from concussion and because I'd been unconscious for so long, which was a bad thing, and because of my age, when complications might set in, they needed to keep me under observation for a day or two.

I also needed three stitches in the cut on my head where I had hit the wall, and treatment for a few bruises sustained when I fell down. As it turned out I was perfectly all right and recovered without any ill effects.

was not until the next day that I heard about Karl.

rs. Williamson came to see me around midday,
ng the usual hospital gifts: fruit, flowers, soft drinks.
e asked me how I was before detailing the events of
ight before. And only then, when, I suppose, she had
ed herself that I was strong enough to bear it, she told
out Karl.

is leg was so badly shattered they had performed an
gency operation, which took four hours to complete,
g which the surgeons inserted a metal pin into his
and repaired the other bones and muscles as best they
.

is mother had been with him when he regained
iousness that morning, and had only come to me when
drifted off to analgesic sleep. The doctors thought the
tion had been a success, but they wouldn't know for
or a few days. Karl was young and strong and fit and
esponding well to treatment, so there was, they'd told
Williamson, no cause for worry and every sign that all
d turn out well.

e reassured each other with the usual bromides: he'd
hrough, he'd be OK, he was in good hands, everything
eing done that could be done.

it our eyes spoke realities to each other, not hopes.
oth knew that every operation is a risk, and doctors
ways optimistic and put the brightest spin on a prog-

we looked at each other, Mrs. Williamson's eyes filled

with tears, she reached out, took my hand in both of hers and held it tight.

In all she had gone through with Karl in the past year, not once during the trauma of his crisis or the relief of his recovery, not once until now had she touched me intimately.

"I'm sorry!" she said, but held on.

"Don't be," I said. "I'm glad you can."

"It's the sight of him lying there like that. Tubes and drips. His leg. Unconscious. Helpless. And not able to do anything."

"Being there," I said.

"D'you think he knows? When he wasn't conscious, I mean. When he's not awake."

"My wife," I said, "before she died. She was in a coma for a while. I was with her all the time. When she came out of it, she thanked me for staying with her. I asked her, I said, 'You knew?' Yes, she said, she'd known. Not like when she was awake but not like in a dream, either. A different kind of knowing. But she knew. She said she knew she was going. But because I was there, she wanted to come back and say good-bye. She died a few hours later."

Mrs. Williamson let out a deep sigh. "We never know," she said. "We don't know everything about life. Or death, come to that. Do we?"

I said with a "that's life" smile, "No, we don't."

She smiled too and gave a fatalistic shrug.

I said, wanting to give her the cue to go back to her

Thanks for coming to see me. And for the gifts. I'm
'm fine. Waited on hand and foot. Having a holiday
"

ll come back later," she said.
ay hello to Karl for me and give him my love."
certainly will," she said.
as sorry to lose her hands.


he day was long. They wanted me to rest and avoid all
ous activity. They had to be sure the symptoms were
ng up and I didn't need a brain scan. The worst of it
hey wouldn't let me read or write because that was
osed to be bad for me too. I realised once more how
arable life would be if I could never read and write
.


rs. Williamson visited briefly that evening. Karl was
ering well. "Sitting up and taking notice," she said.
as still fuzzy from the anaesthetic and the painkillers
were giving him.
he was going home for the night. Would be back
rrow.


ext day was a day of visits.
vice from Mrs. Williamson. The first time, happier,
er, more confident, more like her best self. Karl was
g well.
he second time late that day, less hearty. Karl had

taken a dip. The nurses said it was normal. Postoperative depression. As the anaesthetic wore off the patient was more aware of the pain, more aware of the consequences of what had happened. But Mrs. Williamson felt there was more to it than that. She recognised the signs. Karl had withdrawn into himself, wouldn't talk about what was really bothering him. She was afraid this latest catastrophe might trigger the melancholia again.

Between Mrs. Williamson's visits two others.

The first from Fiorella, in the afternoon.

When I met her at the party, we said only a few words to each other. Not enough for me to gain any sense of what she was really like. People often put on their party persona along with their party clothes, and just as often their persona, like their clothes, is quite the opposite of their everyday self. Which of us would want to be judged by our hair-down hijinks?

Fiorella was certainly got up to kill that day, leaving, as Mr. Cooksley put it, "not much to the imagination," and strutted her stuff to the delight of the rugby youngbloods and the (envious?) scandal of the ancientry. ("I'm glad she's not my daughter," Mr. Cooksley muttered.) I thought at the time, whatever else you could say about Fiorella, one thing was for sure: she did nothing by half.

I say she delighted the youngbloods. But as I discovered later (and report in chapter twenty-four), one youngblood

ot impressed—Karl, for whose eyes, I supposed,
a had dolled herself up in her glad rags (if anything
ensive could be called rags) and to capture whose
on she flounced among the lads. Maybe she hoped
mes of jealousy might reignite Karl's interest in her.
he badly misread her man.


en Fiorella turned up unexpectedly in the hospital,
s subdued and dressed as soberly as a nun.
angely enough, given what she said later, my instant
ht was: She's a performer. An actress. Her emails, I
en, were all performances, voices she was acting out
how they sounded. So who and what was the real
a?
cky told me what happened," Fiorella said with the
f a tragedian. "I thought I'd come and see how you

ery good of you," I said, in the role of the suffering
t. "And to see Karl too, of course," I added, switching
role of the undeceived.
s," Fiorella said, with a quick change from tragic to
But you mainly."
eally?" The question was rhetorical, and offered with
ile of disbelief.
want to explain."
hat is there to explain?"
arl and me."
hat about you and Karl?"

247

Her expression now was of intended seriousness.

She said, "I won't be seeing him anymore."

This was an announcement that worried me. Not for her sake but for Karl's.

"Oh? When was this decided?"

"Yesterday."

"Yesterday? But Karl was out of it most of yesterday. Did you see him then?"

"No. He doesn't know yet. I was going to tell him today, but it wasn't the right time. He's worse than I thought."

"And when it is the right time, what are you going to tell him?"

"That he isn't my type."

"I see! Well, in fact, I don't see. I'm surprised, after all you wrote in your emails."

"I was wrong. I thought he was, but he isn't."

"And this became clear to you yesterday?"

"Yes."

"And what was it you realised?"

"That I'd been pretending."

"Pretending? Pretending what?"

"Well, for a start, that I didn't mind standing in the cold on the touchline while he played rugby when I'm actually not that keen on rugby, and then not seeing him for hours afterwards while he raved it up with his rugby mates. And pretending I didn't mind sitting under a tree all day while he fished and paid me no attention, when I'm not that keen on fishing or sitting under trees all day. Maybe I wouldn't

minded the rugby and the fishing if he'd talked to me
t himself. And if he'd paid me more attention. But I
felt he was really thinking about me. It was always
here was something else than me on his mind and I
t know what it was and he wouldn't tell me. I did try.
's why I gave him the list of questions. And I thought
sked him to write the answers it would be easier for
I'm not that keen myself on talking about myself, but
like writing about myself and I thought he might be
hat too. Big mistake, as it turned out. But how was I
ow he was dyslexic? He didn't tell me, and neither did
other. It might have been different if I'd known. Too
ow, though."

But you must have known all along, about the rugby
he fishing?"

did. But, like I said, I pretended. To myself, not just
im. Because physically he is my type. And there is
thing about him. Like a mystery, a secret, something
al locked up inside. And I really wanted to know what
s. And I thought I could kind of, you know, *unlock*
nd he was keen on me. Very keen. So I thought he'd
e in if I went along with him. So I did . . . Do you
rstand?"

think so. But what happened that made everything
?"

When I went to see him in his shed. His workshop.
ote to you about it."

remember."

"We'd broken it off after . . . the trouble at the camp."

"You'd broken it off, to be accurate."

"Yes, I broke it off. But then I regretted it. I couldn't get him out of my mind. So I thought I'd try again and went to see him. And I told you how I felt like I was being tested. But I didn't know what the test was. Like an exam when you're expected to give the answer to a question you haven't been asked but have to guess."

"I think you're right. You were. Karl is like that. He does test you. He wants to be understood without having to explain."

"I wrote to you about it. And all you wrote back was 'Think artefact.'"

"I did."

"But I couldn't think what you meant."

"No?"

"No. I mean, I guessed you meant it had something to do with the bits of wire I'd seen. But what? I couldn't work it out. You really weren't much help."

"I'm sorry." I lied. I wasn't a bit sorry. If she couldn't work out what I meant, she was right, Karl wasn't her type. More important—which Fiorella didn't seem to have considered so far—Karl knew for sure then, that day in his workshop, that she wasn't his type, either.

"It only came to me what you meant," Fiorella went on, "at the party. You meant the bits of wire had something to do with Karl making something, and Karl was testing me to find out if I understood and what I thought of it."

odded.

nd then it was too late."

odded again. "You'd missed the moment," I said.

Vhat d'you mean?"

ometimes the course of our lives depends on what we
don't do in a few seconds, a heartbeat, when we either
the opportunity, or just miss it. Miss the moment and
never get the chance again."

That's sad."

nd we never forget and always regret a missed
nent."

Are you talking from experience?"

try never to talk from anything else."

he heaved a sigh.

That isn't all," she said.

There's something else?"

Becky."

Becky?"

The girl who was with me at the party?"

I know who you mean. But what about her?"

I brought her with me for, you know . . . ?"

Moral support?"

I was nervous about meeting you and seeing Karl again.
d with a lot of other people. I didn't know what to say to
n or how he'd treat me."

"And?"

"Well, you must have seen. I'm sure everybody did.
w he and Becky got on. I never expected that. I didn't

251

think she was his type at all. She's quiet and studious. A bit of a nerd really. Mad keen on art. To be honest, one reason I asked her was because I thought . . . you know . . . she was . . . safe. But you must have noticed?"

"I did have an inkling."

"Well, she went a bundle on him."

"And Karl?"

"He talked more to her than he's ever talked to me."

"So you decided to cut your losses?"

"I wouldn't put it quite like that!"

"No, sorry. A bit commercial. Blame it on my concussed brain. I'm still not thinking straight."

Another lie. It seemed pretty obvious to me.

"There's just one more thing?"

"Which is?"

"Would you tell Karl for me?"

"Tell him what?"

"That I won't see him again."

I couldn't help laughing.

"Certainly not! You must tell him yourself."

"You wrote those emails for him."

"That was different."

"I don't see how."

"Different or not, I won't make that mistake again. You told me off for doing it, remember?"

"But it's just that I don't want to see him again. I'd say it all wrong. And get upset. And now there's Becky. Who is a friend and I don't want to lose her. And I might if she

I'm trying to take Karl from her. I mean, she really is
⋯n him. She talks about nothing else, which isn't like
⋯ all. I've never heard her talk about a boy for more
⋯bout two minutes before. I thought she didn't like
⋯to be honest. So you do see, don't you?"

⋯see, but sorry, Fiorella. This is something you have to
⋯urself."

⋯e looked miserable and sat in silence.

⋯r the first time, I felt sorry for her. A performer who
⋯'t yet found the role she was meant to play. And at
⋯noment, she was failing at every role she tried on. But
⋯tually, she would get it right. She was a trier. My guess
⋯e is one of those people who are so self-confident, and
⋯o well supported at home, and so admired wherever
⋯go, that they can play around, trying roles out, getting
⋯n wrong, and bounce back without too much hurt or
⋯nage to their egos. The kind of people who always fall
⋯their feet, whatever catastrophes beset them, many of
⋯ch they cause themselves.

⋯And Karl? He was the opposite of that. Which is why
⋯rella found him so fascinating. Fiorella knew without
⋯n thinking about it that, give or take the occasional
⋯ure, she'd always succeed. What she didn't know was
⋯t Karl thought he was nothing else but a failure. (I
⋯ew this because it takes one to know one.) This was the
⋯cret Fiorella sensed was locked up inside him. And what
⋯e didn't know she wanted to know was what it is like
⋯ believe you are a failure and that you always will be.

And what neither of them knew, and Karl needed to know, and I'd learned the hard way, was how to turn his belief in himself as a failure into success. Which is what I'd hoped he was about to discover, and which I worried might now be impeded by the calamity after the party.

Fiorella stood up. "Oh well, I'll just have to write to him and tell him."

"Maybe that's best," I said.

She nodded. "Well, then. I'll say good-bye."

"Good-bye, Fiorella. Best of luck to you."

"I'll still read your books."

"Thanks. I need all the readers I can get."

"Get well soon."

As she walked away, I felt better about her. Beneath all the outward show, her tryout performances, there was a good and sensitive person. She'd had a pretty easy life. Then Karl came along, awkward, wary, passionate and withdrawn at the same time, a combination of physical strength and emotional weakness, of certainty and doubt. She wanted to be loved by him but, for the first time in her life, she couldn't quite capture someone with her charm. Whatever gambit she played, Karl answered with an unexpected move, one of which shocked her and almost caused her to give up the game. But she returned because she couldn't bear the thought of failing and hoped to checkmate him by one final desperate move. Now she had retired hurt. And though she couldn't acknowledge it yet, she would be all the better for it.

…at evening I was told I could get up next day.

…d go home?

…e doctor was concerned because there was no one to

…fter me. So perhaps I should stay another day just to

…sure all was well?

…id I felt fine, no dizziness, no headache—both were

…t I hadn't been on my feet since the "accident." So

…see how things are tomorrow."

…idn't say it, but I had no intention of staying another

…a hospital.

…en Becky arrived.

…e was—I keep using the past tense; I ought to say

…—one of those people who, at first sight, look plain,

…uiet, unassertive, unmemorable even. But who, when

…start to talk and you get to know them, become more

…more attractive and impressive, and you see that in

…hey are beautiful. Not conventionally beautiful, not

…rity beautiful, but beautiful all through.

…Hi," she said. "I'm Becky. I don't know if you remember

…I was at your party."

…Yes, I remember."

…How are you?"

…Fine, thanks. I'll probably be let out tomorrow."

…he smiled.

…Good." And then serious, blushing, "It was awful, what

…pened."

There as an awkwardness about her that was somehow attractive. I'd noticed as she walked towards me that she had feet of the kind that looked as though they'd trip over themselves and make you smile at the sight.

I said, "You've been to see Karl?"

"I've been with him all day. His mother's with him now."

"How is he?"

"All right, I suppose, given he's had a major operation."

"I wanted to go and see him, but they wouldn't let me up. I will tomorrow."

"I wondered about that. He'd like to see you. He's a bit down. Not because of his leg so much but because of his sculpture. He can't bear what they did to it. It's like they destroyed some of himself . . . He doesn't put it like that. He doesn't say it . . . But I can tell that's what he feels. We've tried to reason with him, his mother and me, but it's like he can't hear."

"Or doesn't want to."

"Yes. I haven't known him long. Well, only since the party. But we got on from the first minute. It was like we'd always known each other. We just *fitted* . . . If you know what I mean?"

"I know exactly."

"We talked about his sculpture. Which I think is terrific, don't you? . . . Very like William Tucker's. Karl said you knew Tucker's work."

"Only what I've seen in photos, apart from the one we saw together."

ell, we talked about that and what he wants to do,
e were going to London to see some other sculptures
think might interest him . . . But . . . I'm sorry . . ."

on't apologise. I'm interested."

ell, the thing is . . . You see, I don't know what to say
ill make him believe again. I mean, believe he should
"

that what he's saying? That he won't do any more?"

s."

o, no, no! That won't do. He must do more."

e *must*. I agree." The slightly awkward, slightly shy
er had gone. She was suddenly very passionate.
n we talked at the party, I could tell. It's him.
ture is *him*. It's what he *is*. What he's *meant* to do.
you agree? Don't you?"

, I thought, behind that quiet exterior there lives a
nined mind.

es," I said, "I agree."

knew you would. I just felt you would."

et me think about what to say. And I'll go to him as
as they'll allow me tomorrow morning."

hanks. Thanks so much."

No need to thank me. You're the one to be thanked."

Me. Why?"

or believing in him."

do. But you see, I love him. I haven't known him long.
w hours. But I *know*. I think sometimes important
gs happened to you in a flash. And sometimes it takes

257

ages. And I know people will say I can't know so soon. But I do."

She said this with such matter-of-fact directness, it was utterly convincing.

"And," she said in the same quiet tone, "if you don't mind me saying so, I think you do too. Love him, I mean."

I was so taken aback I couldn't reply.

Luckily, she went straight on. "There's something else."

I waited, still unable to speak.

"If I tell you this, will you promise you won't tell anyone else? No one at all."

"Is it about Karl?"

"Yes."

"Is it bad news?"

"Yes."

"All right. I promise."

"I know one of the nurses on Karl's ward. We went to school together and have stayed friends. She shouldn't have told me but thought I ought to know. She was at a meeting with the ward staff and the surgeon who operated on Karl. The surgeon said Karl would never play rugby again. It would be too risky because of his leg. But they agreed not to tell Karl or anyone else until he's fit again and strong enough to cope with it."

We stared at each other, too upset for words.

All of a sudden, I couldn't bear lying down. My heart was pounding. I had to sit up. I struggled with the bedclothes,

them off, and pushed myself up so that I could sit
edge of the bed.

ky sat beside me, an arm round my shoulders.

ther of us said anything.

en I'd caught my breath and my heart had calmed
I said, "That's not good news."

he reason I wanted you to know is so you'll see why
ore important than ever we get Karl's mind back on
ulpture."

es, yes, I understand."

He has to start sculpting again before they tell him."

ou're right. And you did right to tell me. Thanks."

Between us, and with his mother's help, it'll be OK.
t it? Don't you think?"

Yes, yes. He'll still be able to fish. And once he's
oting and working again, it'll be OK."

Are you OK?"

Yes, yes. I'm all right. It was just a shock."

What about I come to you tomorrow morning and
e you to Karl and then leave you together?"

'Good idea. They are being a bit sticky about letting me
tomorrow. No one to keep an eye on me at home, and
age. All that sort of nonsense."

"I see. Well, if they won't let you walk, I'll take you there
a wheelchair!"

I laughed.

"Oh God! Not a wheelchair!"

"I'm only joking."

"Unfortunately, Becky, all too often a joke tells the truth."

She stood up.

"I'd better go. It's nearly chucking-out time and I want to say good night to Karl."

"Go, go. And good night to you."

"I hope you sleep well."

"Till tomorrow."

"Till tomorrow."

She walked away down the ward and out of sight. And all I could think was how lucky she and Karl were to find each other.

# twen+y-seven
- - - - - - -

ED. PERVERSE. OBSTINATE. SELF-WILLED. BLOODY-
led. Stubborn. Obdurate. Pigheaded. Intransigent.
tumacious . . .

muttered to myself all the words I could think of that
ied my reaction to being woken in my hospital bed at
hirty.

'm always awake at home by that time and usually
by seven. So why resent it in hospital? Because it was
uired by "them." Because I didn't decide for myself;
ey" imposed it on me.

Was I always so bolshy, so obstreperous, so unaccom-
odating?

I smiled as I remembered how at school I wouldn't read
e set books but only other books by the same author or
the same subject instead. And then have to force my
umbling self to mug up the set book at the last minute.

How far back in my life could I trace this intr[...]
I remember as a very small boy refusing to eat [...]
mother put in front of me, and guzzling wh[...]
didn't want me to eat.

"You've always gone against the grain," my mo[...]
said in exasperation.

I was up, abluted, dressed, and sitting impat[...]
the chair beside my bed, plotting how I'd escape [...]
wouldn't let me go by midday, when a nurse hove i[...]
with Mrs. Williamson and Becky, both grinning [...]
With a wheelchair!

"Your friends have come to take you home," th[...]
said in that cheery way they have. "They've promised [...]
after you. And we need your bed for a more deservin[...]

Mrs. Williamson winked. Becky, behind the [...]
back, put a finger across her lips.

I perspired with gratitude.

And we were out of there in five minutes fl[...]
reluctantly in the wheelchair—but I'd have put u[...]
anything no matter how humiliating in order to esca[...]

"How did you do it?" I asked, when we were saf[...]
our way down one of those cubular, vinyl-tiled, anti[...]
hospital corridors that seem designed to make you f[...]
whether you are or not.

"With a little help from Becky's friend," Mrs. Willia[...]
said, "and as the nurse said, by promising to look afte[...]
till you're fully recovered."

"And how do you plan to do that, when you live three miles from my house?"

"We'll talk about that later," Mrs. W. said. "The first thing we have to do is see Karl."

"But it isn't visiting hours yet," I said.

"Mothers have their ways," Mrs. W. said.

"I've met your ways before," I said. "You are a finagling woman."

"You watch your language," Mrs. W. said. "We're taking you to Karl, and leaving you with him for half an hour. That's all you are allowed. Becky and I will have coffee in the café, if you can call it coffee, and we'll fetch you when the time's up and take you home in Becky's father's car. Then Becky will come back to be with Karl while I settle you at home. Understood?"

"Grief!" I said. "You *are* managerial today."

"Stop complaining," Becky said.

"It's the effect hospitals have on me," I said.

"It's the disinfectant," Becky said. "Makes you feel they are about to do something surgical to you. Or it does me, anyway."

"Have they said when Karl can go home?" I asked.

"Not yet," Mrs. W. said.

Becky gave me a look that meant "Don't say any more."

Hospitals are places where we suffer private pain in public. No wonder operations are performed in rooms called theatres. At the same time, they are a kind of prison, which is why the rooms where patients are herded together are called wards. And the nurses, if the one who had just chucked me out was anything to go by, might as well be called warders. (Unless, of course, you have lavish amounts of money and then, as always, everything is different.)

Karl, who hated being on show at the best of times, did indeed look like a prisoner, shackled to his bed by a contraption that suspended his encased leg upstretched in the air as if he'd tried to kick a ball while lying on his back and had got stuck.

His face was a picture of brooding dejection. I remember thinking as I approached his bed: It's not his leg that's making him ill, it's being in hospital.

Mrs. W. and Becky left me by his bedside. We said nothing to each other. But from the moment he saw me he never took his eyes from mine, and that was enough communication between us, knowing each other as we did now.

His eyes said, "Get me out of here."

"They kept me in bed till this morning," I said when it was time to speak.

"Your mother and Becky are taking me home," I said. "They'll come straight back when they've settled me in."

"You're OK?" Karl asked.

"I'm fine," I said. "Concussed. They wanted to be sure it wasn't dangerous. My age and all that guff."

"We'll get you out of here as soon as we can," I said. "You're going to be all right."

"How do you know?" Karl said.

"Medically, you mean? I don't. But you're fit and young and they say they've fixed your leg up good and proper."

"So who does know?" Karl said.

"The doctors. What do they say?"

"That I'll be OK."

"There you are then."

"But I don't trust them."

"Why not?"

"The way they say it. And the way they look at each other and the nurses when they're talking to me. I think they're lying."

"What about your mother? You trust her, don't you?"

"She'll tell me the good news but not the bad. Not while I'm in here. In case I go off the rails again."

"So you feel you can't trust anybody?"

He gave me the hint of a smile.

"What is . . ."

"Is!"

The hint broadened into an actual smile.

"Let's talk about something else," I said. "They won't let me stay long."

"Like what?"

"After the party you said you'd thought of how to make the sculpture better."

He looked away for the first time.

"I'm not doing it again," he said. "Why not?"

"They'll only smash it up again."

"If they do, you'll make another."

"Oh, thanks!"

"But I don't think they will."

"Why not?"

"That sort get bored very easily. No stamina."

"But what's the use!"

"Doing it. The use is *doing it.*"

"So some dickhead can smash it up."

"That's the reason for doing it again."

"For it to be smashed up? Talk sense!"

"You want the world to be left to the dickheads?"

"Course not!"

"Then you're going the right way about it."

"Me! I'm not doing anything."

"Exactly."

"Exactly *what?*"

"You know why they smashed it up?"

"For fun. For laughs. I don't know."

"Because it threatens them."

"Threatens them? How?"

"Because they don't understand it."

"Neither did most of the people at the party."

"Not the way you wanted them to. But they didn't smash it up."

"Only because they know me."

"Give them a bit more credit than that."

266

"All right, so they didn't understand it, but they didn't smash it up. So what?"

"They didn't understand it, but they were trying to. They wanted to. That's the difference between them and the dickheads who did smash it up."

He shifted in the bed, trying to sit up more. Winced with the pain the movement caused in his leg.

I said, "I had a chat with your boss at the party."

"And?"

"You've known him a long time, I gathered."

"Since I was born. He was my dad's best friend."

"Did he tell you what he thought?"

"Not his cup of tea."

"Anything else?"

"It was well made."

"Nothing more?"

"No, why?"

"He didn't tell you he was glad you'd made it?"

"No."

"And how proud your father would have been?"

Karl gave me a suspicious look.

"He said that?"

"He did."

"Really?"

"Really."

He turned away.

Then, muttering: "So you're saying the dickheads smashed it up because they didn't understand it and didn't want to."

"Exactly. And they smashed it up to try and get rid of it. To feel they had won."

He looked at me again. Now his eyes were lively again.

"I'll bet," he said with a grin. "A lot more dickheads around than people who don't understand but want to."

"There are always more destroyers of what you are trying to do than there are people who are on our side."

"Which means they'll always win."

"Only if you stop making. For one thing, the dickheads never manage to smash everything. And for another thing, if you, and the people like you, the true artists, keep on making, the philistines can't smash up everything. There may be fewer of you. *Of us.* But we win in the end."

Silence.

"And even if we don't," I went on after a moment. "Even if they smash everything we make, it doesn't matter, because in making it we give pleasure to people who love us, people who admire us, people who *try* to understand. Like your boss. And your mother . . . And Becky . . . And Fiorella too, you know, whatever you might think about her now."

Another silence. But I could feel his mood shifting.

I took from my pocket the little stone he gave me after we'd built the cairn.

"Remember this?" I said, holding it out in the palm of my hand for him to see.

He glanced at it and turned away again.

"Course. I found it in the river."

"You gave it to me."

"Yes."

"Why?"

"Don't know. I thought you'd like it."

"Only that? We saw a lot of stones that day. Why give me this one?"

"No idea. It just seemed different. I hadn't seen anything like it before."

"What d'you think it is?"

He gave me a huffing look. "A stone with a hole in it."

I laughed out loud.

"What's so funny?"

"You are! You're the one complaining that people don't understand what you're trying to do, but when I show you this, all you can say is it's a stone with a hole in it."

"Get to the point."

"OK. I'll admit, at first, I thought it was just a stone with a hole in it. I kept it on me all the time, because you gave it to me and I valued it for that. I've looked at it a lot. Have a good look at it yourself."

He took it from me, turned it over and over, looked closely at it.

"What d'you think now?"

He was puzzled.

"Dunno."

"D'you think it's just a little stone that got like that

naturally. Smooth and perfectly round, and the hole dead centre?"

"Could have done."

"But you're not sure?"

"No. It feels . . ."

"What?"

"That it was made like that."

"Exactly the conclusion I came to. So I did some research."

He eyed me, knowing now I had a surprise in store.

"And?"

"I suspect it's a marriage stone."

"A what?"

"A marriage stone. You know how we give rings when we marry? Well, I think this is a very old version of that. Prehistoric, probably. Thousands of years old. Made by a man to give to the woman who was his wife. She probably hung it round her neck."

"You're not kidding me?"

"No, no. I can't be sure. But I asked someone who's an expert on that kind of stuff and he told me that's what it could be."

He looked at the stone again. Pushed his little finger through the hole, and showed it to me as if it were a ring, and laughed.

As I did too.

"A made thing," I said. "And the man who made it doesn't have a headache anymore, that's for sure. But now we have it. And even now, thousands of years after it was made, it still gives us pleasure. But more than that, when you picked it out of the river you knew, you knew instinctively, it was something different, something special. And you gave it to me. Why? Not just because you thought I'd like it."

He shook his head.

"Level with me," I said.

"All right! OK! A kind of thank-you."

"Which you were too upset that day to say?"

"Probably."

"Which I knew at the time and appreciated. You didn't need to say it. The stone said it better. Just like I imagine it said more to the lover of the man who made it than he could say in words."

He looked at me hard.

"You needn't go on," he said. "I get the point."

"Exactly. No need to say it. But seeing it's a marriage stone, I think you'd better have it back and keep it for the right person on the right occasion, don't you?"

He laughed. "I'll find something else to give you instead."

"You don't have to. You've already given it to me. It's in my front garden. In pieces, yes, but ready to be put back together. And even better than before."

He nodded and looked away, back to the little stone, which he fingered in his hand.

We were silent again.

Until I said, "Becky came to see me. She's quite

something."

He nodded.

"Studies art history."

He nodded.

"I'll tell you what. Ask her about the oldest sculptures in the world and where they are. And then ask yourself how they've survived, just like that marriage stone, for thousands of years, if it's true that the dickheads always win."

Silence again.

Becky and Mrs. W. arrived at the door of the ward.

"I've got to go," I said. "But you know what?"

"What?" Karl said, full face to me again.

"This talk about giving up, and not making any more sculpture, it's not you talking."

"Who, then?"

"Your leg."

He smiled, full and bright, his eyes alive again.

"I'll be back this evening," I said.

I got up and turned to go.

"When you come . . . ," he said.

I turned to face him.

"Yes?"

"Bring some paper and a pencil, will you?"

"Anything else?" I said.

"Some of that wire I use, if you have any."

"No problem," I said.


On the way home we stopped at the nearest supermarket

272

and stocked up with food for me and for Mrs. W.

I didn't let on that I suddenly felt physically weak doing even this undemanding chore. Maybe, I thought, the docs and nurses were right about me being careful for a few days.

Back home, the rods from the sculpture were still scattered around the garden. A forlorn sight. As soon as we had opened up the house, switched on the heating and checked that all was well, Becky collected the pieces of rod and stored them in the garage.

While she was doing that, Mrs. W. prepared a pan of soup, ready for me to heat up at lunchtime.

The first thing I wanted before anything else was a shower. Why is it that hospitals, which are meant to be astringently clean, make you feel grubby and sticky?

Mrs. W. insisted on waiting till I was dressed in clean clothes before she allowed Becky to drive her to her own house, where she wanted to pick up some things for Karl. They both insisted they would call to see me again later, for which I was grateful. I felt wobbly and vulnerable, perhaps unconsciously fearing I might fall down and damage myself again.

When they'd gone, I toured the house, relieved to be among my own things in my own place.

I sat in the reading chair in my workroom. But didn't read. I wanted to rest, breathe myself in again, so to speak. Didn't want to lie down. I'd had enough of that in hospital.

I thought of everything that had happened in the last few days. And this extended, back and forth, over the events since Karl first came to see me.

And I knew it was time.

I moved to my desk. The desk on which I've written all my books. I've never been able to write them anywhere else.

You must go on making, I'd told Karl.
You can't let the philistines destroy you.

What was true for Karl was true for me.
You mustn't allow even death to destroy you.
And it can't if you live in what you make.

I looked at the photo of Jane, which has always stood on my desk. And I knew what she would say.
If you can't do it for it for yourself, do it for me.

I took from my drawer a new refill pad made of recycled paper, with faint narrow ruled lines and four holes in the margin for filing. I've always used them for drafting my books.
I took a new 2B pencil. The kind I always use.
I wrote the date and time at the top of the page. I always

do when I start a day's work.
    And began.

    "Could I talk to you?"
    "Why?"